Comments from Readers and Reviewers

"From the beginning, I wondered how Blake was going to find the young soldier who killed his father and what he was going to do once he found out. The conclusion of the story was not what I expected, but it was even better and I liked it very much. Viewing the war from a child's perspective, a member of the army no less, gave me a new understanding of what really went on during the Civil War." **Readers' Favorite 5-star Review, Lorena Sanqui, reviewer**

"The new book will appeal to young teenagers who are interested in learning a little more about the Civil War as seen through the eyes of one of their peers. Blake's experiences are based upon extensive historical research and are rooted in the actual movements and actions of the regiments involved in the storyline. The book flows well and should be easy to read and comprehend for its intended teenage audience. Rated at four or five stars by various on-line reviewers, it would make a fine gift for the younger Civil War reader." **Scott Mingus, reviewer, author of Civil War non-fiction research**

"I really like how it ends and how Blake finds out about Matthew." **Daniel Esh, Jr. age 12**

"This one really tugs at the heart. I could imagine my son all the way through this story. To see in my mind what Blake (my great-grandson's name BTW) was going through in the way of situation and the hardships involved allowed me to get closer to the real experience. This was a horrific war that reached out to every US citizen in some way but to see it through a child's eyes was a very different experience and a very impressive one. This is really one to read if you have any interest in the Civil War. It gives insight into the real experience." **Amazon Review by Iris A. Coffin.**

"I loved the book about Blake. I like the part about when Blake gets kidnapped." **Steven Lee Stoltzfus age 9**

"The final revelation where Blake and Matthew discover the truth about their connection is an incredibly powerful moment, arguably the defining point of the story." **Hollywood Coverage, recommendation for a Feature Film, Xlibris review team**

"I very much enjoyed following Blake's quest to avenge his father's death. After suffering the deprivations and horrors of war, so clearly portrayed, he apparently came to the realization that his anger was more justifiably directed toward the brutality of war rather than toward his father's slayer. The upstanding character, affability, energy and resourcefulness that Blake displayed in his dealings with those with whom he came into contact, should serve as an inspiration and role model for young readers." **Stan Stubbe, reader**

The regiments and their histories in this story are real, the events did happen.

BLAKE'S STORY
REVENGE AND FORGIVENESS

written by
J. Arthut Moore & Bryson B. Brodzinzki

created by
Bryson B. Brodzinski

Blake's Story: Revenge and Forgiveness
3rd Edition - Colored Copyright © 2019
by J. Arthur Moore and Bryson B. Brodzinski
3rd Edition - B&W Copyright © 2019
by J. Arthur Moore and Bryson B. Brodzinski
Revised 2nd Edition Copyright © 2017
by J. Arthur Moore and Bryson B. Brodzinski
Original Copyright © 2014
by J. Arthur Moore and Bryson B. Brodzinski

ISBN:978-621-434-121-4 (softcover)
978-621-434-122-1 (hardcover)
978-621-434-123-8 (eBook)

All rights reserved.
No part of this publication may be reproduced, stored in a retrieval system, or transmitted in any form or by any means - electronic, mechanical, photocopy, recording, scanning, or other – except for brief quotations in critical reviews or articles, without the prior written permission of the publisher.

This is a work of historic fiction. As a blend of fact and fiction, the names, characters, places, and incidents either are the product of the author's imagination or are references to actual persons, events, and locales, blended within the context of the story, through research.

Printed in New York by:

OMNIBOOK Co.

OMNIBOOK CO.
99 Wall Street, Suite 118
New York, NY 10005
USA
+1-866-216-9965
www.omnibookcompany.com

For e-book purchase: Kindle on Amazon, Barnes and Noble
Book purchase: Amazon.com, Barnes & Noble, and
www.omnibookcompany.com/journeyintodarkness/

Omnibook titles may be purchased in bulk for educational, business, fundraising, or sales promotional use. For more information please e-mail info@omnibookcompany.com

Designed by: Gian Carlo Tan

Author's Notes

The concept for this story was first suggested by Bryson Brodzinski, the 10-year old great-grandson of author J. Arthur Moore, on April 3, 2013. Pictures were taken, a character name was selected, and on the following day, Bryson began the prologue for the story. The two planned to email the story back and forth as it was developed. But Bryson's busy schedule prevented this from happening.

On a trip to North Carolina in February 2014, which was to include a photo shoot at a historic plantation, Bryson laid out the story's plot line, typing his thoughts in a word document. It would open with a letter, which Bryson wrote, then continue according to the created plot outline. Acknowledging Bryson's heavy schedule of school and soccer, Moore would take this material along with the previous material, research the history, and draft the story. As it developed, pieces would be emailed to Bryson for editing.

The History

The regiments and their general officers incorporated into this story are real. Their involvement at Shiloh, Richmond, Perryville, and Stones River did happen, mostly as depicted in the story. The details from the battles are researched and factual. The research included books as well as web sites. The actions of the fictitious characters are based on real events or imaginary events that could have happened. Where the research sources were not available, the story evolved around what could have been based on the times and the facts that were known.

As the reader follows Blake's story, the reader will be living history through Blake's experiences.

DEDICATION

Blake's Story, Revenge and Forgiveness is dedicated in love and with pride to Bryson Brodzinski, creator, co-author and greatgrandson to author J. Arthur Moore, who asked that the story be created and that he could be a part of it and help with its creation. It is also dedicated to Jonathan Wilkins, Andrew Sellman, Isaac Sassa, Andrew Wilkins, Austin Nedrow, Ethan Blazek, Ryan Nedrow, and Connor Blazek who have become forever a part of the story by representing the boys within the story, and to all those who dream of writing, to say to them – follow your dream. Lastly, it is hoped that the reader will enjoy the story and know that it is one boy's dream come true.

Photography

All photography is by the author, J. Arthur Moore.
Blake Bradford is represented by J. Arthur Moore's 10/11-year-old great-grandson.
Bryson Blake Brodzinski, who helped to create and co-author the story.
Matthew Mills is represented by Andrew Wilkins, the author's 18-year-old neighbor.
Tyler Chase is represented by Andrew's brother Jonathan Wilkins, a drummer in
the Pequea Valley High School's marching and concert band.
Aiden Larken is represented by Andrew Sellman, a volunteer period character at
Hopewell Furnace National Historic Site.
Todd Johnson is represented by Isaac Sassa, grandson of a board member of the
Friends of Hopewell Furnace, the first student to write reviews for the author's works.
Christopher Jamison is represented by Austin Nedrow, a drummer in
the Field Music, 1st Pennsylvania Volunteer Corps.
Beverly McDonald is represented by Ethan Blazek, a junior member of
the model railroad club to which the author belongs.
Timothy Sanderson is represented by Austin's brother Ryan Nedrow, a fifer/bugler in
the Field Music, 1st Pennsylvania Volunteer Corps.
Jimmy Dickson is represented by Connor Blazek, Ethan's brother.

Settings for the photography include

The author's back yard
Historic Brattonsville, a southern plantation at McConnells, South Carolina
and
Hopewell Furnace National Historic Site near Elverson, Pennsylvania

Contents

Comments from Readers and Reviewers i
Title Page iii
Author's Notes v
The History v
Dedication vi
Photography vii
Blake Bradford xi
Tyler Chase xiii
Aiden Larken xv
Todd Johnson xvii
Matthew Mills xix
Christopher Jamison xxi
Beverly McDonald xxiii
Timothy Sanderson xxv
Jimmy Dickson xxvii
Map Blake's Journey, July to February 1862 xxix

The Story

Prologue 1
Chapter One 3
Chapter Two 21
Chapter Three 39
Chapter Four 57
Chapter Five 77
Chapter Six 105
Back Album 129
References 139
    The Kentucky Campaign 1862 140
    Army Organizational Chart. 141
    The History Behind Blake's Story 142
    Sources 148
About the author - J. Arthur Moore 150
More Comments and an Email 152

BLAKE BRADFORD

TYLER CHASE

Aiden Larken

TODD JOHNSON

MATTHEW MILLS

CHRISTOPHER JAMISON

BEVERLY MCDONALD

Timothy Sanderson

Jimmy Dickson

- xxvii -

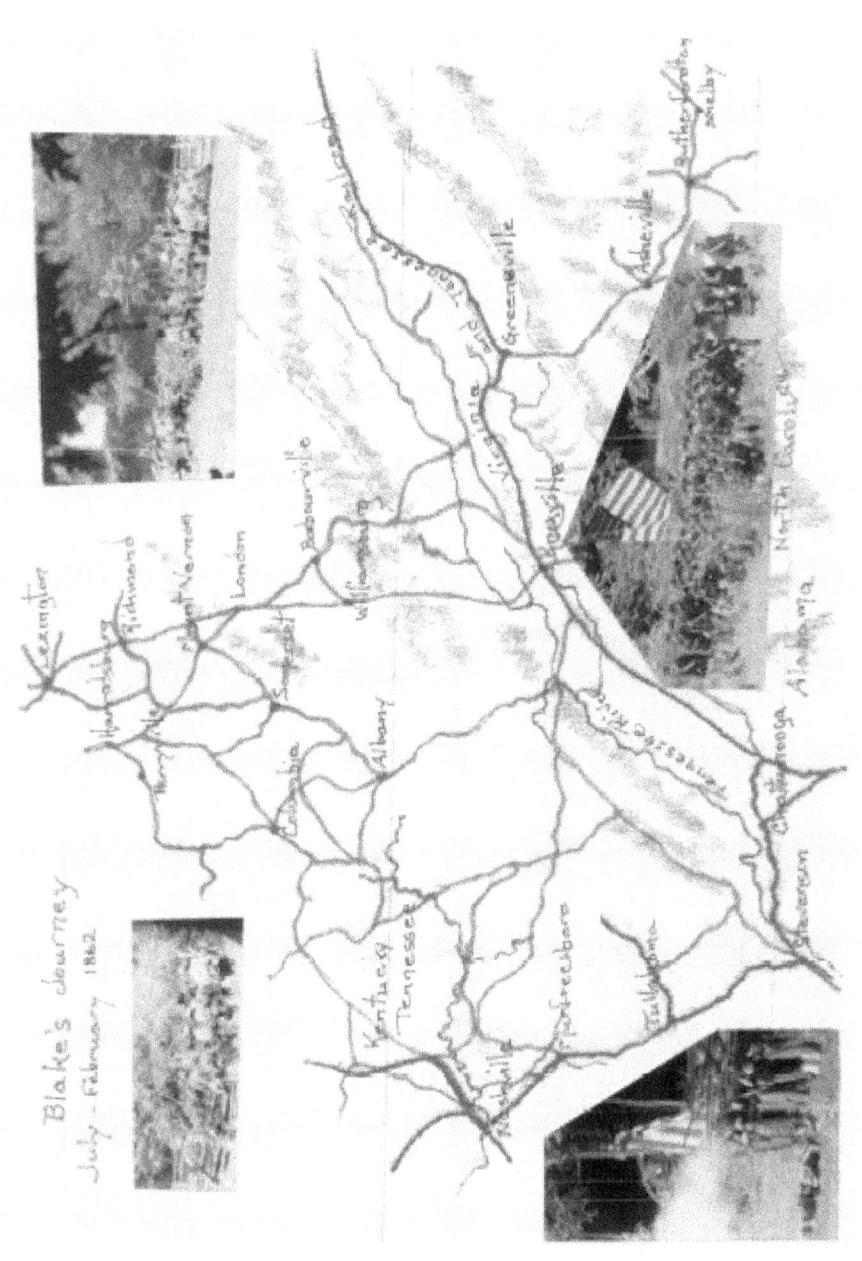

Map Blake's Journey, July to February 1862

Prologue

"Colonel, what the heck is going on?" Blake asked Colonel Butler. Colonel Butler answered roughly, "Son, you are in a war."

Blake looked out into the battlefield. "Wait, how did I get in the…" He paused. A bullet flew overhead.

Chapter One
The Letter

Corinth, Miss.
April 9, 1862
Mrs. Micah Bradford
Bradford Plantation
Shelby, NC

Dear Madam,

During the battle at Shiloh our soldiers attacked a line of Union soldiers. Captain Micah Bradford was struck down by a federal soldier. He was struck in the head and died instantly. After the battle he was buried on the battlefield. We assure you that we will send his personal affects to the plantation.

I remain yours,
David H. Cummings, Col., 19th Tennessee

The letter came as a thunderbolt. It was the last thing the family expected. Blake's mother stared at the paper as if it were not real. "How could this happen? Micah had just written that all was well, the weather was wet with unending rain, but he and his friends in his Tennessee regiment were doin okay."

For Blake, the news was as a storm that tore him apart. How dare an enemy soldier hurt his father, how could an enemy soldier kill his father. This just could not have happened. He would have to do something about it. He would have to avenge his father's death. Yes, he would go to the war and kill that soldier.

* * *

It all started in April of 1861. Seven southern states had seceded from the Union to form The Confederate States of America. In Charleston, South Carolina, officials had demanded that the Federal forces surrender Fort Sumter, which was set in the harbor. Instead, President Lincoln sent a shipment of supplies to the fort for its existing garrison of troops. Thus, in the early hours of April 12th, Confederate batteries of artillery opened fire on the fort with a bombardment lasting into the following day. Lincoln called for 75,000 volunteers to help put down the rebellion. War had begun.

"The horses are ready to plow the fields," Father said.

"Father, is it time to plow the fields?" Blake asked.

"Yes, son, it is time to plow the fields," said Father.

Blake answered excitedly, "Yeh, I love working in the fields!"

Micah Bradford and his 10-year-old son Blake frequently worked in the fields near the big house, not because they had to, but because they enjoyed the time together. The Bradford Plantation had three dozen slaves for the fields and another dozen for the house. Today, the two would turn the soil for the household vegetable gardens. They covered over two acres of ground because they grew a large variety of vegetables, spices, and herbs for the household kitchen needs. Slave families had their own garden plots near their brick slave quarters. The Bradford Plantation had its own brick kilns where slave craftsmen made the bricks used for the buildings of the plantation.

Micah led the team from the stable area to the field, where the plow lay nearby. Blake brought the plow from its resting place to the edge of the field and helped his father hitch it to the team.

"We're ready, Son," his father stated. "You take the reins and I'll follow close behind so I kin reach 'round ya and guide the plow."

It was a warm April day as father and son worked the quarter-acre garden plot to be planted with potatoes. Blake adjusted his straw hat to keep the sun out of his eyes. His father paused to lift his hat and mop his head with a large bandana. About halfway through the plot they moved on to the end of the furrow closest to the house where a young houseboy, Sammy, waited with fresh-made lemonade.

"Mas'ers, my ma says ta see ya have som'thin cool," Sammy offered as he held the tray for each to take a glass.

"Sammy, ya tell Sarah as we mightily appreciates her thoughtfulness." Micah placed his empty class on the tray. Blake soon followed.

"Yes, Sir," the boy replied as he turned back toward the house.

Finally, the last furrow was plowed and it was time to put things away. Charlotte Bradford, Blake's mother, walked over from the house to admire the garden and wait for the men to return from the barn. Celia and others of the slave women along with their younger children would put the crop in tomorrow.

After Blake and Father finished plowing the fields, Blake heard gunshots.

Blake asked Father curiously, "Father why do I hear gunshots?"

Father answered roughly, "Get inside!" He whispered to Blake's mother, "They're coming!"

"Who's comin?" Blake asked, wondering if he should be scared.

"Hot-headed abolitionists who have been causing trouble ever since Lincoln was elected," his father explained as the three dashed toward the back porch of the house. Sammy met them at the door with their muskets.

"Sammy," the man instructed, "run over ta the south field and tell Jackson ta bring the hands in, there might be trouble."

The boy ran off to do as he had been told.

The three younger Bradford children came running to the door from within the house.

"Father, what's happenin?" nine-year-old Raymond called excitedly.

"I think the abolitionists are coming ta cause trouble. Ya children and yer mother stay inside while I go out front ta see what's up." Micah took both muskets and walked through the house to the front porch.

The thirty-three-year-old plantation owner stood resolute at his full five foot and ten, determined that these ruffians would not harm his family. But he needn't to have worried. Sam Henderson, Kris Miller, and several of his friends and neighbors came charging up the pike with guns blazing in some sort of celebration.

"Micah," Sam called above the noise. "A rider jest come in from the east with news! Some a ar people fired on Fort Sumter in Charleston Harbor and Lincoln has declared war!"

The riders reined their horses to a halt at the front steps. Charlotte and the children rushed out from the house. Sarah, the house servant, was with them. Astonishment shown on their faces.

"What!?" Micah exclaimed. "are ya sure? I knew it might happen, but really didn't expect it would."

Kris added, "We're ridin on ta spred the word. We have ta gather an he'p Davis ta recruit an army."

"Ya kin meet here," Charlotte offered. "We kin be ready with dinner fer tomorrow."

Micah added, "If it works fer ever'one, pass the word."

"All right with ever'one here?" Kris asked the other riders.

"Yeh." "Fine with me." The riders chorused.

"We'll pass the word fer tomorrow at noon," Sam stated.

"Let's ride," Kris added.

"See ya'all then," Micah waved.

The riders turned north and set off up the road. The temporary quiet was once again punctuated with gunfire as Jackson and the field hands arrived from the fields. Micah shared what had just happened and all set about readying the plantation for the following day's gathering.

* * *

Blake pushed his blond curls out of his eyes as he placed his broad brim felt hat on his head and rummaged through his wardrobe in search of his drumsticks and strap. The drum was on the floor beside his bed. Ever since neighboring states had created the Confederate States of

America, his music teacher had been teaching the boy how to play the field drum. Blake's drum was a gift from his teacher, a relic from the Mexican War. Now he would play it to welcome the day's gathering to a planning session for the war effort. Found them.

The boy fastened the strap across his shoulder and stuck the drumsticks in the pocket of his blue wool pants, also a gifted war relic. Picking up the drum from its place on the floor, he started for the hallway and down the stairs to the center hall below.

"Blake." His father called as the boy descended the staircase. "Why don't ya go out on the front porch beside the steps where ya kin play as people arrive."

"Yes, Sir," he acknowledged as he left the room and stationed himself near the top of the front steps.

The people came by the dozens and Blake played for them as they entered the house. They wore their best clothing as if to a party, and some came in uniform. The gathering collected in the large parlor room where several spoke about preparing for the war.

Micah addressed the crowd. "Friends. We are gathered here ta prepare ta fight fer ar state's defense an ar rights ta live ar lives without interference. We will defend ar lands an ar families 'gainst foreign invasion. True, North Carolina hasn't yet declared, but many 'spect she will. As we raise ar companies an create ar regiments, I will also be goin ta the aid of a friend in 'nother state. I will take a company of volunteers ta Washington County in eastern Tennessee where ma friend, Jason Clarkson, is he'pin ta gather a regiment in a countryside full a Union sympathizers, but where many are workin hard ta gather troops fer the Confederate Army an need whatever support you and I kin offer. Again, Tennessee hasn't yet declared, but is expected ta. Others here will be puttin tagether companies ta he'p fill the ranks a North Carolina's regiments. Sam Henderson is organizing troops fer here in Carolina. Kris Miller will be recruitin volunteers fer ma company ta leave fer Tennessee by mid May. Over the next hour, git yerselves organized so thet afta today, ya kin gather in yer units an make preparations.

"After that, ar people have prepared tables and dinner out on the lawn, after which there will be music an dancin on the porch and in the center hall. Now ta business, then ta pleasure."

As the day wore on, companies were organized, plans were made, dinner was served, music and dancing followed, and the gathering dispersed as the late afternoon sun drifted toward the hills. The household staff cleared the meal, cleaned the dishware, and put everything away. The field hands broke down the tables and cleared the yard. As people departed homeward, Blake once more drummed them on their way.

Micah stood on the porch by his son as the last of the carriages pulled out onto the roadway. The drum went silent. Blake felt a hand on his shoulder and the comfort of a gentle hug.

"Ya did a fine job, Son," his father complimented.

"Thanks, Father. It all seems so excitin, but I wish ya didn't have ta go." The boy felt a sense of pride, yet also a pending sense of loss.

"Son, I, too, wish this war had not come. I don't want ta be away from ma family. But it shouldn't last very long. I 'spect ta be back in time ta harvest the crops in the fall."

Charlotte stepped out onto the porch. "Micah, if it's okay with you I'll dismiss the staff fer the night. Ever'thin has been cleaned up and a fresh pot a coffee is on the stove in the kitchen. The other children are playin in the back yard."

"It's okay. We'll be in soon's I make ma rounds." To his son he said, "Leave yer drum inside by the staircase. Would ya like ta walk the rounds with me as I check on ar people?"

"Yes, Sir." There was a sense of pride at being asked to walk the evening rounds.

Blake left his drum, sticks, and strap at the bottom of the staircase in the front hall and returned to walk with his father, down the steps and across the yard toward the outbuildings and the slave quarters, on the evening rounds, to make sure that all was well with the plantation for the night.

* * *

In the weeks that followed, Blake and his father continued to work the garden fields and finished preparing them for planting. Celia and the household women and their children put the crops in and cleaned out and freshened the spices and herb gardens. Their men folk worked on the flower gardens as Mrs. Bradford supervised the plantings of annuals and the care of the shrubs and roses. The field hands cultivated the plantation's fields and planted the crops of corn, wheat, oats, flax, tobacco, and cotton. Spring butchering was done and meats were salted down and hung in the smokehouse for the weeks ahead. Women went to work making uniforms for the troops, and munitions and supplies were acquired for the companies along with wagons and horses as needed.

During this same time the family followed developments from newspaper articles and news carried by travelers and post riders. Virginia left the Union in mid April. Lincoln established a naval blockade around the Confederate states by the third week of April.

April was drawing to a close. The last of the fields were being prepared.

"Marse Micah, come quick!" Jackson's 14-yea-old son James dashed toward the house as fast as he could run. "Steven's hurt bad in the tobacca field!" He stopped at the back porch out of breath.

The family rushed out the door to see what the commotion was about. "What happened?" young Ruben asked. The six-year-old was the first out the door.

"He was walkin beside the plow and throwin the stones thet turned up when he tripped an fell 'gainst the blade."

"Is your pa with him?" Micah asked as he followed his young son out the door.

"Yes, Sir."

"Then he'll be okay. Is the wagon out there?"

"Yes, Sir."

Celia came out after the family. "Celia, get some bandages and go with James. James, put him on the wagon fer Celia ta tend an drive 'em back. We'll set up here on the porch an Sarah will take care a him when ya git back."

Celia returned from the house with a sack of bandages and followed James back to the field.

"Charlotte, have Sarah git her medical kit and tell Sammy ta bring some water. Blake, if ya an yer brothers and sister are gonna watch, stand aside out a the way." The four moved back against the railing.

Micah stepped down off the porch and walked toward the field to meet the wagon. Fifteen minutes passed before the sound of the wagon's wheels grinding on the gravel path, could be heard. It paused briefly while Micah peered at the damage, then moved on toward the porch.

"How's it look, Celia?" the man asked.

"It's cut deep, Marse. It bled bad, but Jackson tied it off." The wagon approached the porch.

"James, what's that on his leg?" Blake asked, looking at a bandage with a stick twisted through it and tied off.

"My pa calls it a turnicut," the older boy replied.

Young Steven cried in pain, "It hurts bad!" Tears streamed down the 11-year-old's face. "Please, he'p me!"

"It's gonna hurt a while," Micah stated as he lifted the boy from the wagon and carried him to the porch where he laid him on the floor. "Sarah knows what she's doing. She's bin doctorin the folks a this plantation fer nigh ta twenty years now."

"What's a turnicut?" Blake asked.

His father explained. "It's when ya put anythin ya have 'round a wound an tie it as tight as ya kin 'til the bleedin stops. Usually ya have ta put a stick through it as Jackson did and twist it tight an tie the stick so it can't unwind. It's usually a wound where an artery is cut and it bleeds like a fountain an ya'll die if it's not stopped. Ya need ta fix the cut as soon as ya kin an take the tourniquet off b'fer the lower part of the body dies from lack of blood."

Steven began to calm some as Sarah started to work on his leg.

"Kin Sarah do thet?" Blake's little sister Ruth Ann asked.

Her mother answered. "Watch. Sarah will wash the wound so she kin see how it is, sew it together, and put a tight bandage on it ta hold while it heals."

All watched quietly as Sarah worked her medical magic. The children had not seen this done before and were awestruck. Steven, too, was fascinated by what the servant woman was able to do for him.

"We'll put a bed in the kitchen fer Steven where Sarah kin keep an eye on him. When he heals and she kin cut out the stitches he'll go back ta his quarters," Charlotte announced. "Now that she's finishin, James kin go git a straw pallet from the shed an put it on the porch here fer Steven ta use durin the day."

As James went for the pallet and Sammy helped his ma clean up, the family prepared to return to the house while Celia helped Steven to sit up against the porch railing.

A rider approached from the lane.

"Hello the house. Anyone home?"

"Daniel!" Micah called. "'round back."

"Uncle Daniel!" the children chorused as they ran from the porch and surrounded his horse.

"I didn't know ya was comin," Raymond called. "How long kin ya stay?"

Daniel Bradford dismounted and handed the reins to Blake. "Yer father asked if I would like ta run the plantation while he's away, so I turned ma store over ta ma head clerk an came ta check it out."

"Where ar yer thin's?" Ruth Ann asked.

"One a ma freight drivers is bringin 'em over an should be here some time tomorra."

"What happened here?" he asked spying young Steven on the porch.

"He had a accident," Ruben offered.

"Come in, Daniel," Micah invited. "Blake will take care a yer horse and we'll have coffee an somethin ta eat. The children kin tell ya 'bout the accident. Then we'll ride the plantation an git acquainted with what has ta be done."

The family retired to the house as James brought the pallet and helped Steven to settle in, and Blake took his uncle's horse to the stable.

"I caint stay. I have ta take the wagon and git back ta the field. Sammy'll be out ta stay with ya. I'll tell yer pa how ya is an he'll be ta see ya when work's done."

Sammy brought a glass of lemonade from the house and sat with his friend as James climbed aboard the wagon and turned it back toward the fields.

* * *

It was Friday, May 10th. Tennessee had seceded on Tuesday. Micah's company of eighty men and officers was arriving at the plantation to encamp for the weekend to drill and prepare for departure on Monday for the 10-day journey from Shelby to Telford's, Tennessee, to join Jason Clarkson's company and move on to Knoxville where the regiment was assembling. The air was filled with the dust of arriving soldiers and wagons, as they pulled off the pike and were directed to locations on the front lawn to set up their camp. The Bradford children and those of the household staff watched the activity from the front porch, while the colored men and older boys helped with wood and water supplies and locating wagons and picketing the horses. The women folk worked to keep the house clean from the dust and to prepare food to feed the men.

Tent lines took shape in rows running north and south, parallel to the pike. A broad company street ran down the middle with about sixteen small shelter-half tents on either side. Larger officer and supply tents were set up at the south end of the company and kitchen tents and dining canvass were at the north, nearest the lane off the road and the plantation outbuildings. Wagons and horses were also located at the north end of the camp.

As the camp took shape, the children left the porch and began to wander and mingle with the soldiers, ask questions, and offer to help. Blake wandered to his father's tent where Jackson was setting up its interior.

"Are you and James excited 'bout goin?" the boy asked.

"I don't like leavin Mary behind, but know she'll be a he'p with the crops as she's knowin what needs doin." He turned from assembling and making up the captain's cot. "James, he'p me put the captain's desk tagether."

The two placed the wood horses and placed the desk on top, then opened the camp chair in front.

"Yer pa's a good man, Blake. James and me are proud ta go with him and will see ta all his needs. Ya rest easy. Taylor will take good care a thin's in the fields an on the plantation. Yer uncle has taken charge quickly an yer family is in good hands."

"Who's the boys in the fust tent outside?" Blake asked.

James responded as he paused from placing the captain's trunk beside the desk. "Tyler Chase is the drummer fer the company and Robert Connell is the fifer."

"I kin play the drum and have learned some on the bugle, too."

"Ya have ta be twelve ta be a musician. Tyler's thirteen and Robert's fourteen." James stood to survey the tent and be sure all was in order.

"James," his pa instructed, "we have ta meet Lieutenant Miller at the wagons and make sure all the supplies is in order. We'll see ya later, Blake." The two left.

Blake wandered out to the musicians' tent. The boys had finished laying out their blankets and were arranging their packs and gear at the back of the tent. Blake watched, envious of their uniforms, as they finished and came around front.

"Hi, I'm Blake," he introduced.

The boys responded, "I'm Robert." "I'm Tyler."

"Kin I play yer drum?"

"Sure," Tyler replied offering the drum strap.

Blake adjusted the strap, fastened the drum, and took the sticks Tyler offered. The young drummer struck up a lively march, impressing the older musicians. Robert took out his fife and added a lively tune to go with the drum cadence. The three enjoyed sharing their music for several minutes. Nothing was said. When they had finished, Blake handed the drumsticks back to Tyler and placed the drum and strap at his feet.

"Yer good," Tyler complimented.

"I've been drummin fer the gatherin's. Wish I was old 'nough ta jine ya."

"Yer the captain's son, he kin take ya now."

"Naw, he said he wants me ta home. It's too dangerous."

"Maybe we'll see ya when yer older," Robert offered. "Come back afta supper an we kin play some more. Bring yer drum"

"Thanks. I'll do thet." Blake turned to join his brothers and sister and explore more of the camp. The musicians placed their instruments beside their tent and wandered off to check on friends.

As he wandered the camp, Blake learned that many of the soldiers were friends and neighbors his father's age with their teenage sons. Others were young men in their twenties and a few older men, some with previous military experience in the Mexican War. He liked the noise of the camp, the smell of smoke from newly lit campfires and of new canvass from tents being put up for the first time, and the general feel of excitement and adventure that seemed to fill the air.

Taylor led a crew of field hands who set up the long tables in the area of the cook tent, where the company would eat while in camp. Once they left for the march, rations would be issued to mess groups made up of small groups of soldiers who would cook on the fires at their tents. The noon meal was served by the household staff. The children returned to the house to eat with their families. They described for Steven all that was happening on the front lawn. After they had eaten, they arranged to move his pallet to the front porch where he could watch.

* * *

Blake got permission to move into his father's tent for the weekend. He enjoyed time with the musicians and being able to play with them throughout their stay in camp. Tyler and Robert made him an honorary musician, even securing for him a pair of grey wool uniform pants, which Celia altered to fit, and a uniform forage cap.

Saturday was spent in drill and musket practice and the hills echoed with the thunder of their volleys as the company's squadrons fired in line. Their guns were not military issue, but the ones the men brought from home, most being farmers and skilled hunters. Some of the guns were old flintlocks. Lieutenant Kris Miller was in charge of supplies and spent his time making sure all kitchen, food, and camp equipment and supplies were accounted for and extra cartridges and caps were on hand. These were gathered in the main supply wagon. Another would remain empty until the camp was struck and would contain the headquarters tents and furnishings as well as the kitchen canvass and related poles and equipment. Finally there was the kitchen wagon with all its food supplies, cooking utensils, large water barrel on the side, and strapping underneath for firewood. Each soldier would carry his own gear, including half of the tent.

On Sunday afternoon, the families of the soldiers were hosted by the plantation and many of the younger boys were permitted to tent with their fathers for the last night. Families gathered with their men folk around a large bonfire that night. Following taps by the drummers, they gathered on the porch or downstairs rooms to be with the soldiers come morning, to watch the encampment activity as it was packed up, and to bid the company farewell as it headed to Shelby and points west.

On Monday morning, May 13th, the camp was struck and packed for the journey west and north into eastern Tennessee. When all was ready, families gathered for tear-filled farewells. It was a time of crying and warm embraces as Micah's family said goodbye. Mary wept as she hugged James and Jackson in order, then stood back bravely to watch them on their way. James and Jackson were teamsters for the headquarters wagon. Coloreds with the other officers were teamsters for the remaining wagons.

Blake stood at the road and played his drum as the company marched in formation from the plantation property onto the pike. Tyler and Robert struck up a lively tune for the march and nodded to Blake as they passed. The younger boy paused as the company passed, first to salute

THE LETTER

his father on his golden stallion, Prince; then his friends, the musicians. Micah acknowledged with a crisp salute and a smile sharing the pride he felt for his son and for his troops. No words were exchanged, tears said it all. Tyler and Robert nodded in their acknowledgement of a friend of equal talent, just not old enough to go along. The wagons rumbled by bringing up the rear.

A gathering of families with tear-streaked faces watched silently as their fathers and brothers marched proudly up the pike to turn west toward Shelby, toward war and an unknown future.

* * *

Two days later the letters began. The first night out Captain Micah handed a letter to the local post rider to be delivered to the plantation. Always they contained the news of the day, the places they passed, and words from Jackson and his son for Mary. They traveled west from Shelby through Rutherfordton then Ashville, then northwest into Tennessee at Greenville. There they were able to take a train the rest of the way to Telford's. The march was easy at first, but quickly became difficult as the company entered the mountains of western North Carolina and eastern Tennessee. By week's end they had crossed into Tennessee.

On the following Tuesday, May 20th, North Carolina seceded from the Union.

* * *

The 19th Regiment, Tennessee Infantry was assembled at Knoxville, Tennessee, during May and June of 1861 as the companies gathered from the counties of the eastern mountain areas. Micah's friend, Jason Clarkson was with Company B from Washington County. Micah's company became Company J.

The months ahead included garrison duty at Cumberland Gap. Summer slipped toward fall. On September 18th, a small detachment including Companies B and K saw action at Barbourville, Kentucky, where they captured a Union training facility and its meager store of supplies. Micah wrote that they had remained in Kentucky, managing a couple of successful raids to acquire supplies, but were suffering a great deal from an assortment of diseases. Nearly half the men in the regiment were unfit for duty. One who suffered greatly was James. His father's devoted care managed to enable him to recover.

In October there was action in Tennessee near Cumberland Gap and Bowling Green as Unionist guerillas became active and burned several railroad bridges. After bringing control to the region, the 19th returned to Kentucky by late November.

Micah wrote home in late November, "We have crossed the Cumberland and set a camp at Beech Cove near Mill Springs. A large Union force has gathered in front of us, but we have a river guarding our flanks and strong defenses to our front. Yet we continue to suffer from disease."

In December he wrote, "Our Brigade commander, General Zollicoffer, continues to hold us in this position, though it is beginning to look dangerous as the river rises. Still he refuses orders to move us. A new commander is being sent to replace him."

Winter set in. The situation at Beech Cove Camp grew more dangerous.

The Letter

Beech Cove Camp
Kentucky
January 22, 1862
Mrs. Micah Bradford
Bradford Plantation
Shelby, NC

My Dearest Charlotte and Children,

This past Sunday at about 11:30 at night, we set off to attack the enemy come dawn. Marching through mud, sometimes a foot deep, we encountered their pickets around 6:00 in the morning. We, along with the 15th Mississippi, engaged them in a running battle for nearly a quarter mile. Believing we were firing on our own troops, General Lollicoffer charged ahead to stop us. But he was mistaken and charged right into the Union Army. Some of us had started to follow him, but he was killed, so we fell back. Our Colonel Cummings was put in charge of the brigade and tried to correct our battle lines. But our artillery support was ineffective and so many of our troops were still using their old rifles, many of them flintlocks, and they misfired due to the wet in the air. We retreated to Camp Beech Cove and were ferried across the river by the steamboat, Noble Ellis. With the Federals in hot pursuit, General Crittenden ordered the boat burned so they couldn't use it. We had to abandon our stores and have few provisions.

James has recovered and he and Jackson send their love to Mary.

I remain your loving husband,
Micah B. Bradford, Cpt, Co J, 19th Tennessee

After reaching Gainesville on January 26th, the brigade was resupplied. Two weeks later it moved to Camp Fogg near Carthage, then on to Murfreesboro, Tennessee. There the brigades were joined with Albert Sidney Johnson's Army. In letters that followed, Micah enabled the family to follow the movements of his regiment.

Johnson marched his army south into Alabama while considering an invitation from General Beauregard to join a new army he was putting together to go after the Union army in western Tennessee. Along the way, some of the troops were issued new Enfield rifles, but the 19th received reconditioned rifled muskets, still they were better than what most of the men had brought with them. Johnson accepted the invitation, so on March 15th, they left Decatur, Alabama, to join Beauregard at Corinth, Mississippi.

Meanwhile, life marched on back at Bradford Plantation. The holiday season was festive as Daniel Bradford oversaw decorations and bountiful meals. The harvest had been good. With the help of the field hands, the needs for the year were stored and the surpluses were sold. Cotton and tobacco crops brought good prices to sustain the family for the year ahead. It was a joyous season of family warmth and celebration for the slaves as well. December slipped into January slipped into February. February 24th was a very special day, with celebration and gifts. It was Blake's eleventh birthday. How he wished his father were there to celebrate with him.

The 19th joined General Beauregard's army on the 20th of March. Toward the end of the month, Father wrote that preparations were underway for the biggest battle yet as the army was gathering to attack the Union Army at a place to the north called Pittsburg Landing. The weather had turned wet and there were constant rain storms turning the roads to muck and causing a number of forced delays. His troops in the 19th were doing okay. The movement north was immanent and he wouldn't be able to write for a few days. He would write afterwards to tell them what all happened

Then the letter came.

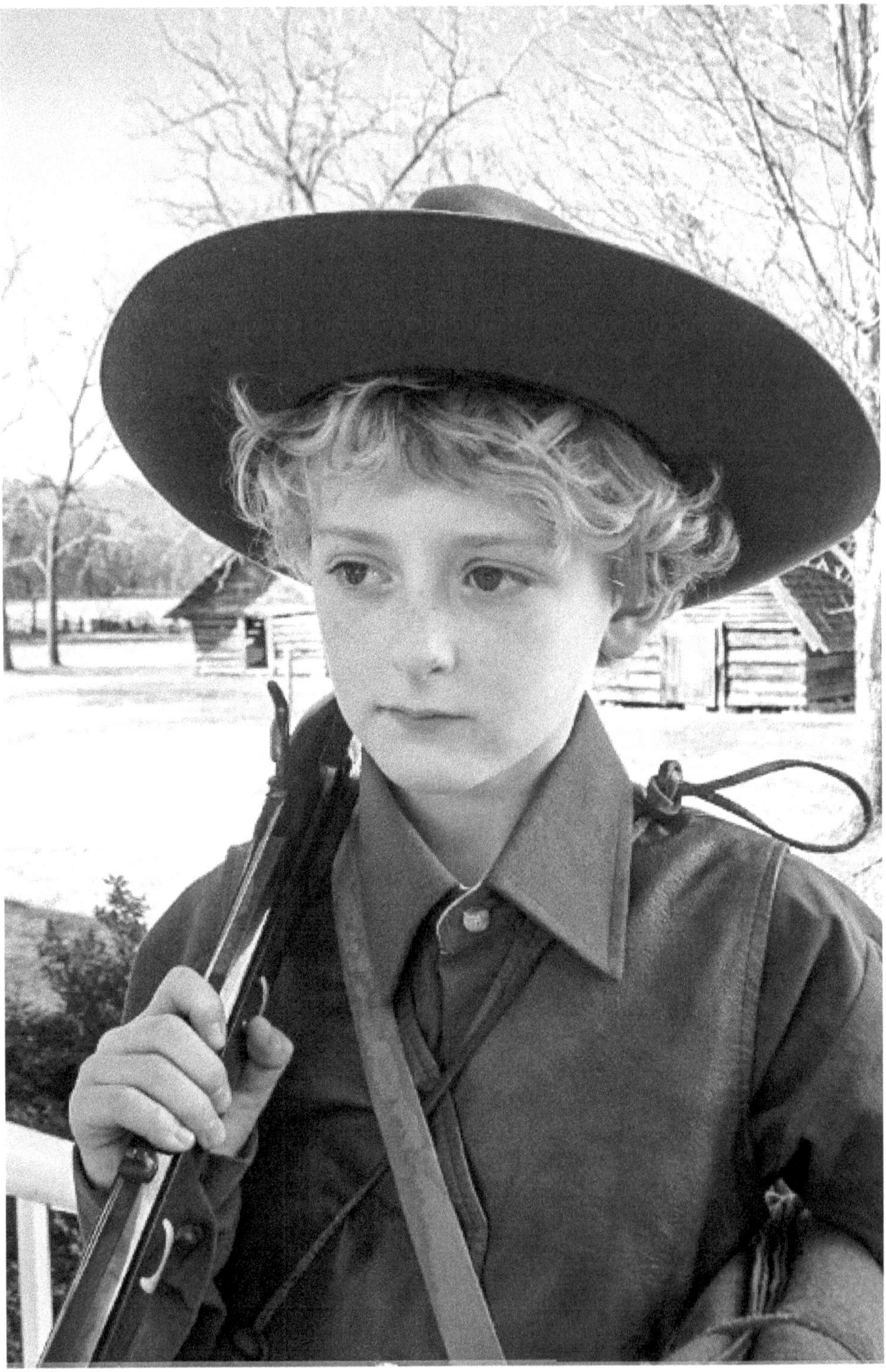

Chapter Two
To The War

A few days after the colonel's letter arrived, another arrived from Lieutenant Miller describing what happened at Shiloh.

Corinth, Miss.
April 10, 1862
Mrs. Micah Bradford
Bradford Plantation
Shelby, NC
Dear Madam,

I know you have been informed of Micah's death. I am so very sorry. As he was killed on the first day of the battle, our army had control of the grounds and burial of our dead was at a cemetery near the Shiloh church. The graves of the known are marked and they can be removed to their homes after the war, if desired. I have secured a small wagon and collected all his personal affects in it. His horse, Prince, survived the battle and will be sent home with the wagon. Jackson and James are being released from the service to bring Prince and the wagon home. Passage is being arranged by railroad from Corinth to Greeneville, Tennessee. From there they will finish the journey by road. They should be safe on the train, but it is advised that someone meet them at Greeneville. They will leave here tomorrow and should be in Greeneville by the 15th.

Now I will attempt to share the circumstances of the battle. We were first sent to scout for Federal troops to our rear. There were none. We were then sent to the front to support the attack on the Federal position which came ta be called the Hornet's Nest where the enemy was putting up a fierce fight. At about 2:30, we attacked the position in great force and were driven back taking several casualties. Again we attacked. It was the third time, getting within ten yards of the enemy, that the captain was hit. He was fighting dismounted having left Prince with the wagons. As close as we were to the enemy, I could see a young Union soldier take aim and fire. He seemed but a boy. I tried to shoot him, but he dropped too quickly behind their defenses and we were soon back from their line. I will never forget his face. The bullet passed through the captain's head killing him instantly. Some of the men who saw him go down, rushed to his aid, but he was already dead. They carried him back to our lines and saw to it that stretcher bearers took him to the rear. Corporal Johnston went with them to make sure the captain's body would be kept for us to tend when the action was finished.

We stormed a cabin and took the woods to the west of the field, then were sent back to our brigade. We were with Breckinridge as the position fell and the Federal soldiers surrendered. As we disarmed them, we were able to exchange our muskets for the Federal Enfields.

We had the Union camps and plenty of food and supplies that night. Later, we buried the captain near a close-by church, placing a marker on his grave.

*I remain yours,
Kris Miller, Lt. Co J, 19th Tennessee*

Daniel Bradford had read the letter to the family. No one spoke for several minutes, each turning his own thoughts over in his head.

"I wanna go ta Greeneville with Uncle Daniel," Blake announced. "I wanna bring Prince home."

The request caught everyone by surprise.

"I don't think yer mother would allow that," Daniel stated when the moment of surprise had passed.

"Daniel, I think it might be a he'p fer the boy," Charlotte responded. "But take some others with ya fer pertection."

"Yes, M'am. I'll take a wagon an some from the store, with supplies ta stop 'long the way at night. I'll send a rider ahead ta tell Jackson ta wait fer us. If he gits there accordin ta this letter, he'll be there tomorra. We need ta go ta Shelby tanight and leave come mornin."

"Kin I bring ma gun?" Blake asked. The gun was special. It was a gift from his father on his tenth birthday. It had been hand-crafted with brass fittings and decorations, and was just the right length for the boy – as long as Blake was tall.

"Yes. Pack what cartridges an caps ya have an we'll git more from the store. Charlotte, I'll need a gun as well. Now let's you an me git packed an on the road, Blake."

The two quickly threw together blankets for bedrolls and stuffed some extra clothes into a carpet bag. Celia packed some smoked meat and biscuits in a flour sack while Charlotte went for the gun.

"Raymond," his mother instructed, "go saddle two horses an bring em ta the back porch."

"Yes, Mother." He was off. Sammy went with him.

Within the hour, Daniel and Blake were mounted and on their way to Shelby. They would spend the night at Daniel's store after preparing a wagon and some of the store staff for an early departure the following morning. As the two riders headed out the lane and disappeared down the pike toward the town, Charlotte and the younger children watched from the front porch.

* * *

"How much longer, Uncle Daniel," Blake asked.

Daniel checked a piece of paper on which he had written some notes and directions. "We've bin on the road three days since Asheville. We should be there by nightfall."

The party consisted of a wagon with two drivers, carrying supplies and camp kit, and Daniel and Blake on horseback. The wagon was covered with canvass and lightly loaded with room inside for the four to sleep on the road if the weather were rough. Most of the trip was clear and they slept outside near or under the wagon. Camps were set late and left early to cover as many miles as possible each day.

A train's whistle was heard in the distance.

"We must be there," Daniel announced. "I hope all's well with Jackson and James and we kin start back fust thin in the mornin."

"I'm hungry," Blake groaned. "I hope there's a place ta git lots ta eat."

Mitch, one of the drivers, volunteered, "I understand thet with the railroad, there's usually a hotel with good food."

"We'll check fust thin," Daniel stated. "Okay, Blake?"

"Yes, Sir." There was relief in his voice.

The party began to pass by houses that were closer to each other, with barns, out buildings, and small fields. They soon found themselves within the surrounds of a small town with some shops and businesses, approaching the station of the Virginia and Tennessee Railroad. The train they had heard was gone. Two box cars sat on the siding. An unattended wagon was parked near the freight depot.

"Pull up by thet wagon, an I'll check inside on Jackson an his son." Daniel dismounted, turning his horse over to Blake, and heading for the door to the station.

The door to the freight depot opened.

"Boy are we glad ta see ya'll." It was Jackson, looking very worried. He crossed the platform to Blake and the drivers. "The train got us here okay, but we was delayed a couple times cause bridges were out and had ta be repaired. We bin here 'bout three days."

"Sure am glad ta see ya too," Blake added as he dropped to the ground and ran to Jackson. James came out and the reunion was complete. There were hugs of relief and the joy of being together again after so many months.

"Are ya both okay?" Mitch asked.

"We are now, Sir," Jackson replied. "We have written orders an a letter a safe passage from Lieutenant Miller with all tickets paid, an some cash fer food 'long the way. But when we got here there was some as wanted to take us as runaways and sell us ta the 'thorities. Marse Daniel's letter was here with the station master an with that and the orders from the Lieutenant, the station master kept us here in the freight depot fer yer arrived."

Keenan, the other driver, spoke up. "Blake, yer uncle said we kin git som'thin ta eat at the railroad hotel. I think we should keep ar wagon here with Jackson's an we should stay here the night, too."

The door to the station slammed shut as Daniel stepped out to cross the yard area.

"I see ya all found each other." He approached the group. "The station master told me a yer problems here, Jackson, an what he's done by keepin ya in the depot. We'll all stay here the night an leave fust thin come mornin."

"What about food?" Blake spoke up from where he stood beside James.

"Jackson an James 'll stay here with the wagons. We'll go ta the hotel fer dinner an bring extra back fer them."

"I'll put the horses up with the team and Prince at the stable," Jackson offered. "James'll he'p"

"Okay, see ya soon," Daniel acknowledged.

While the four turned toward the hotel, the field hand and his son began unhitching the team in preparation for taking the four horses to feed them and bed them down for the night.

* * *

Daniel Bradford and his small group set out early on the morning of the 22nd for the return trip to the plantation. With mixed feelings of sadness and pride, Blake put his saddle on Prince and tied the horse he had ridden to the back of the wagon. He rode his father's horse home. They were safely home by the end of the month. Mitch and Keenan dropped off with their wagon upon reaching Shelby. The other four and the remaining wagon continued home to the plantation. There was great relief from all on the plantation at their safe return, but great sadness at the absence of the captain and his company.

The following evening, after the work day was done and the slaves had returned to their quarters, Blake went over to talk to James and his pa. They sat together on the front steps in the comfort of the evening air.

"Jackson, what was it like?' the boy asked.

"Most a it was marchin, campin, drillin, an waitin. Wust of all was the sickness. James was real sick fer a time an 'bout half the company was sick most a the time." Resting his elbows on his knees, the man gazed out across the yard. "Very little time was actually spent in battle. The drivers was kept behind the lines ta he'p the litter bearers ta bring in the dead an wounded. Mostly we done all right. Some was wounded, no one kilt."

James joined in. "Shiloh was the wust. It rained so much a the time an we was marchin in the rain an mud. Ther was a heavy thunderstorm in the middle a the night the day b'fer the fight. We was bivouacked on the open ground with no cover an ev'one was soaked. Finally near mornin it stopped an we was able ta dry out durin the day. When the fightin started we was sent ta he'p the litter brigade ta carry in the dead an wounded. Pa was there when yer pa was brought in. He he'ped later with the buryin." The boy stopped and there was silence, only the tree frogs chattered in the night.

"Thanks, James," the boy whispered. " Are Tyler and Robert okay?"

"Tyler was wounded at Shiloh by a explodin shell. He lost his right foot an was ta be sent home when he could travel," Jackson informed. "Robert was with the litter brigade an away from the fightin. Jeb Olsen's son, Kimberly, was killed. He was shot in the chest an died two hours later. Kenton Morton and his son both died in Kentucky from disease. Half the comp'ny's still sick, but they fought anyway."

"Was Tyler with ma father when he was kilt?"

"Yes, he an the lieutenant was jest near his right. They both saw it happen. Tyler was hit as the company was fallin back fer reassignment." Jackson looked to the boy. "Are ya okay?"

"Yes. Thank ya fer tellin me."

They all sat in silence. Blake hung his head and cried softly. James, too, was struck with a sudden sadness as a silent tear slipped down his cheek and he brushed it aside with the back of his hand. Jackson looked to the sky and kept his emotions inside.

"Jackson," Blake asked, "kin I talk ta James an ya from time ta time 'bout what happened?"

"Yes. Wheneve ya needs ta talk, ya jest says so."

"Thanks." The boy stood. "I'll be goin now."

Blake walked toward the house as James and his pa sat and watched quietly. As the boy climbed the steps to the back porch, they stood together and watched the sky a moment as the velvet blackness from the east began to chase the last light of the day toward the western horizon. Then they turned and climbed the steps through the door for the night.

To The War

* * *

    Daniel had provisioned Blake with a hundred rounds of cartridges for his rifle for the trip. It was packaged that way and he decided that Blake could use the extra for hunting. He had previously had three dozen rounds of his own. On the second day back, the boy started planning for his journey of revenge. He set aside the hundred rounds in a leather cartridge bag and put it in the back of his wardrobe along with the blanket roll from the trip. He found an old back pack from the storage shed and began to collect things he'd need. The first to be packed were the grey uniform pants and the forage cap. He would take his drum sticks and strap, but not the drum, too much to carry. They would be packed later. He hoped that after Tyler was back, he could come and spend time at the plantation and teach Blake all the drum calls he would need. The boy was no longer the young kid from a year ago when the company first left. He was older and wiser and would be careful not to give any hint of what he planned to do. The boy would follow the war in the newspapers and in the conversations of adults, careful to learn where armies were and how to get to them. He would follow the reports written by reporters who had been at Shiloh and learn the details of the battle and the identity of the soldiers and units who had fought against his father's company. When he knew all he needed to and conditions were right, he would simply leave and tell no one what he was doing.

    The week after returning from Greeneville, Blake started his preparation. It was early afternoon and dinner was finished.

    "Mother, kin I ask James an his pa ta take me huntin so I kin be better. I wanta he'p some by bringin in food fer the fam'ly. Uncle Daniel's become the man a the house, but I wanta he'p, too."

    "I'll talk ta them tonight an see if they kin take ya on Saturday," his mother replied. Charlotte was proud of her son's interest in taking on responsibility.

* * *

    The loud crack of the rifle echoed across the hills. The rabbit stood up and looked in the direction of the noise, saw the boy, then hopped leisurely off into the underbrush. James and Jackson doubled over in laughter as Blake stared dumbfounded in the direction of the missing rabbit. Then he, too, cracked a smile and began to laugh.

"I sorta missed, huh," the boy smiled.

"So bad the rabbit had ta check ya out," James laughed.

"Okay, Boys," Jackson put in, "we got some work ta do ta make a hunter outa this boy."

"Ever shoot thet thin?" James asked.

"Bottles off a stump," Blake replied, "an not so good neither."

"Guess not," Jackson added. "Thet rabbit set there like a bottle b'fer ya took yer shot.

"Here, let me show ya how ta keep yer gun steady an true," he added as he guided Blake's hands to place his gun firmly against his shoulder with his left under the barrel at a balancing spot that was comfortable for his reach.

"Now hold thet there an feel the balance." The man stepped back to allow the boy to sense the feel of the gun placement. "Okay, now take yer gun down, walk a piece, an stop an put it back up."

Blake did as he was told.

"How's it feel?" the teacher asked.

"Good."

"Now reload."

The boy took a fresh cartridge from his cartridge pouch, tore it open with his teeth, poured the powder down the barrel, then pushed the ball and paper in on top. Taking the rammer from under the barrel, he shoved it all down, then replaced the ram rod. Taking a cap from his cap box, he placed it on the nipple under the hammer and eased the hammer down.

"Ready," he announced.

"Purdy good," James complimented. "Ya could git faster. Not likely yer game's gonna wait, but somethin else might show b'fer yer ready."

"Good idea," Jackson added. "Now let's go quiet-like ta the next medda. I've seen some small game there last week."

The three walked slowly and quietly to the low stone wall and hedgerow of scrub growth that divided the meadows. Being early May, new leaves were on the scrubby trees and colorful wildflowers were in bloom in the fields. Their fragrance perfumed the air. It also tended to dull the scent of the hunters to the hunted. They stopped at the hedgerow to carefully survey the next field for any sign of game before proceeding.

"There," James pointed. A buck and two doe were grazing not far from the stone wall, off to the left about twenty paces.

"We'll all take a target," Jackson whispered. "Blake, shoot fust. James an me will folla."

Carefully the three raised their guns and pulled back on the hammers. The loud clicks seemed to fill the air and the buck looked up. Blake pulled the trigger and the rest followed as the hills echoed with the sounds of gunfire. The buck dropped, the two doe ran.

"Great shot, Blake!" Jackson shouted.

"But I was shootin at the closest doe," the boy exclaimed.

"Oh. Let's take a look." Jackson led the way.

James got to the deer first and examined it for bullet holes. "Ther's three," he announced. "One hit its hoof."

"I know which one thet is," Blake smiled.

"Thet's all right. It kept him from runnin so's we could finish him." James smiled at the thought. "Ya'll git better."

Jackson knelt by the animal's side, pulled his hunting knife, and slit open the belly. He reached in and pulled out the deer's insides.

"It's called field dressin," he explained. "Ya have ta clean out the insides a the kill ta keep it from startin ta go bad. Now we need ta pick a pole from the fence line an carry it in. We'll hang it outside the smokehouse ta skin an butcher, then Celia kin pick what she wants ta fix fer dinner an we kin hang the rest inside ta smoke."

"Here," James offered pulling out his game bag, "put the liver an heart in here. The rest kin lay fer the buzzards."

Jackson took his knife to cut a pole from a young sapling in the fencerow while Blake and James bagged the heart and liver, then pulled out a pair of leather ties and tied the buck's fore legs and hind legs in pairs. The three paused, looking at the blood and gore on their hands.

"Wipe them on the grass," Jackson instructed.

They did. It was better, but still felt sticky. Blake couldn't wait to get home and wash up.

Jackson slipped the pole beneath the ties and the deer was hefted to his and James' shoulders.

"We'll take turns," James told Blake. "An when we gits back, 'member, we all shot it."

They all laughed.

The deer was taken up and the three headed back across the low stone wall toward the buildings on the far side of the hill beyond the field.

* * *

 Over the next weeks, gunfire could be heard near the cotton field behind the slave quarters as Blake practiced each day to improve his accuracy and speed of reloading. On Saturdays he would go hunting with James and his pa. On their second trip he finally got his rabbit. By the end of the month the boy could knock a squirrel from its tree. Jackson complimented Blake on his improvement and James asked his pa if Blake was good enough that the two of them could go hunting without him. By June, it was just the two of them. The boy asked his uncle to order more cartridges and caps.
 In the meantime, Blake followed the war in the papers and in any conversations he overheard from the adults. A Union army was working eastward across Tennessee. A Confederate army was following in a parallel direction to the south. Blake asked his uncle if Tyler were well enough to come visit and spend some time on the plantation. He would find out. His music teacher continued to teach him what he knew of military drumming, and when that seemed as good as it could get, he taught the boy how to play the bugle and the fife. Blake preferred the bugle.

* * *

 Friday, June 13th, was a day of excitement and anticipation. Tyler was coming to visit and spend a week at the plantation. Blake had written and asked him to bring his drum so the two of them could play together. Tyler liked the idea. Of course he would.
 Blake sat in a porch rocker on the large front porch of the house, watching to the south for Tyler's approach. A cloud of dust rose through the trees and drifted north up the pike. The boy watched as it came into view and followed the fence line along the pike. He watched it up the roadway and into the front lane. Tyler waved and Blake waved back. The carriage crunched to a stop.
 The black driver hopped down and went around to the side to open the carriage door. Reaching inside, he took out a pair of crutches and stepped aside as the young boy, now fourteen years old, worked his way from his seat to the step to the ground. The driver positioned himself to help if needed, but he knew better than to lend a hand. Blake stood transfixed as he watched the older boy work his way out, hopping on

one leg, the right pant leg hanging empty at the bottom with the lower portion pinned up to keep it from dragging. Knowing Tyler had lost his foot was not the same as seeing it for the first time.

"Blake," Tyler called, "come an git ma drum."

The boy rushed down the front steps to the carriage. Knowing he could not touch his friend to help him, he stood aside until Tyler was on the ground, then reached in and took the drum. The driver handed Tyler the crutches, then went to the back of the coach and took out his trunk. He took the trunk to the front hall where a house servant would take it to Blake's room.

"Thank ya, Bristol," Tyler said as the man crossed the porch.

He paused. "Yes, Marse Tyler. I'll be back Friday next ta pick ya up."

He nodded and was gone – down the steps to the carriage, then out the lane toward the pike, then back south toward the Parker Plantation where Tyler's pa was head carpenter.

Blake set the drum by the door and the two went to the rockers to sit and visit.

"What was it like?" Blake asked. He turned his rocker to better see Tyler as he spoke.

"Well," the older boy began. "The march from Shelby was the easiest. From Asheville we was in the mountains and it were hard. We met up with the captain's friend an he already had a comp'ny, so we b'came ar own comp'ny. Ther was many comp'nies from other towns in the mountains an we was ta meet in Knoxville ta b'come a reg'ment. We was officially mustered as a regiment on June 11th."

The boy paused, trying to decide where to continue. "When did ya start fighten," Blake asked.

Tyler picked up his story, "There was some action in eastern Kentucky in September, but we weren't in it. There was a rebellion in eastern Tennessee in October and some railroad bridges was burnt. We he'ped ta end it. We went back ta Kentucky an set a winter camp. Many were gitten sick from disease by then an it got worst. Nearly half the regiment was sick. Many nearly died. Some did die. In January we got in a fight with Union forces and got pushed out a Kentucky."

"The lieutenant wrote how ya went from there and ended up at Shiloh," Blake volunteered.

"Yeh, an most all thet time till then we did no fightin, only bein sick an movin from place ta place."

"I thought it'd be excitin," the younger boy stated.

"It sure ain't excitin. Very borin. And when ya does git inta a battle, it's horrible killin like ya neve seen b'fer. I's sure glad ta be home an wishes we was all home an this war ain't neve happened." The voice stopped and Tyler sat in silence, a look of forlorn sadness in his eyes.

For a moment, Blake wondered if he were making a mistake and should forget about going after his father's killer. But the thought passed and he was as resolute as ever.

"Ya wanna go see Jackson an James? They was sent back from the war with father's thins and his horse. They're teachin me how ta hunt an he'p feed the family." Blake watched his friend's face for a reaction. For a moment longer, nothing was said.

"Yes, the walk would feel good." Tyler stood and balanced on his crutches.

"Let's see Sammy fust, go through the house an git some cool lemonade." Blake led the way to the door.

"Good idea," Tyler agreed as he struggled to his foot and crutches and they turned to enter the house.

* * *

The lively beat of the drums echoed off the buildings of the plantation and bounced in repetition until it sounded like an entire regiment was assembled.

"Thet sounds neat!" Tyler said. "It sounds like the whole army is here!"

"Wow!" Blake exclaimed.

They paused. It was Saturday morning and the first time the two boys had strapped on their drums and played together. Children and grownups alike came dashing from the house and fields and outbuildings to find out what was happening.

"What is all thet racket?!" Charlotte called as she ran out the back door.

Jackson rushed over from the barn. "It's jest ar drummers gittin some practice," he called. "You boys should warn folk a'fer ya scares us so."

The boys smiled meekly, "Sorry."

"I like it!" Sammy called running from the house.

"Me, too!" Raymond and Ruben chorused from the back porch.

"Kin ya do some more?" Sammy asked.

"Ya might wanna play softer," Daniel suggested.

"I'll tell ya what," James added. "If there was any trouble come on, it'd surely bring ever'one in from the fields."

"James, yer right," Daniel acknowledged. "Ther's bin some abolitionist trouble 'round here lately. What's the drum signal fer callin ever'one tagether?"

"It's called assembly and sometimes the long roll," Tyler stated. "It sounds like this."

He nodded toward Blake and the two struck their sticks to the long roll. The continuous rolling sound of the drums echoed between the buildings and off the distant hills. It went on for minutes but sounded much longer. Then silence.

All marveled at the noise of it.

"Jackson," Daniel called across the yard, "let's agree thet if there is any trouble, we have Blake sound the long roll and all are ta come ta the main house. And Blake," he continued, "ya neve play it agin 'less ther's trouble."

"Yes, Marse," Jackson agreed. "Yes, Sir," Blake chorused.

"Ever'one back ta work," Daniel instructed. "An ya boys practice more quietly."

The yard cleared except for the younger children who settled on the porch steps to listen to the boys and their drums.

"This one's called Reveille," Tyler announced to their audience. He and Blake exchanged nods and began the beat.

Sammy and others of the younger slave children joined the audience as it swelled to nearly two dozen, seated on the porch and the ground at the foot of the steps.

Blake and Tyler regaled their young audience with all the calls they both new. Then the drummer would play a new call and Blake would pick it up and they would play together. By mid day the two were ready for something else. Since it was Saturday, Blake asked, "Ya wanna go huntin with James an me?"

"I'll only slow ya down," Tyler answered.

"There's no hurry. It'll be somethin differnt ta do tagether. We'll stay ta the medas where's it's less hills."

"Okay," the older boy agreed.

After dinner Blake went to his uncle to borrow a gun for Tyler, then to the barnyard to find James. The three headed off to the meadows across the pike where the land was less hilly and hiking would be easier.

No game was taken. It was just good to be together.

* * *

The week drifted on lazily. Most mornings the two boys could be found in the yard playing their drums. Their audience varied from day to day depending on what the younger children were involved in doing. Afternoons varied. There was hunting and fishing, and on occasion there would be chores the two would help to do. In the evening they were likely to be found with Jackson and James, recalling the war and sharing news of what was currently known. At night, they shared Blake's room and reminisced about the time they had shared together during the day and personal thoughts and concerns. Blake told Tyler how he wished he could go to the war and kill the soldier who killed his father. Tyler said that it was a bad idea, he would likely get killed himself, and there was no way of finding that soldier anyway.

Friday arrived. Bristol was due mid day to take Tyler back home.

"I wish ya didn't have ta go," Blake complained.

"Me too," Tyler agreed. "It's been such a great time tagether. I ain't neve felt so good since I bin back. I hope we kin do it agin a'fer long."

They sat in the porch rockers. Tyler's trunk and his drum were on the floor near the steps. Raymond and Ruben sat on the porch steps so they could be near their older heroes. They sat quietly in whispered conversations, saying little to the older boys.

They became aware of a noise in the distance, at first indistinguishable. The boys listened carefully and suddenly knew what it was.

"Gunshots!" Tyler announced.

"Trouble!" Blake added. "Quick! To the back porch! Ruben, go tell Uncle Daniel and Mother. Raymond, take Tyler's drum!"

Tyler grabbed his crutches to pass through the house to the back porch. Blake grabbed his drum from where it rested in the kitchen. The younger boys ran to do as instructed.

In moments the older boys were on the back porch and the long roll echoed through the hills. Gunfire crescendoed as the riders came closer. Sammy brought the guns that Blake and Tyler had used for hunting and the boys set down their drums to be sure they were loaded and ready. They could hear in the distance beyond the buildings the commotion of the field hands rushing toward the house. Charlotte armed the house servants with guns from her husband's gun cabinet in the library. They gathered in the center hall to await Daniel's return from the fields along with the field hands.

The riders approached the lane and turned in toward the house, guns blazing. There were more than two dozen, some old, some young, all looking fierce and ready to kill and destroy. Charlotte stepped out the door, Blake and Tyler on either side, their guns at the ready.

"Ya ain't got no cause ta be here like this," she shouted.

"Nothin ya kin do lady. Yer men folk is off fightin the war. We's gonna take care a the war here." He deliberately raised his revolver.

Tyler's reflexes were faster. In one smooth motion, he threw his rifle to his shoulder and fired. To the astonishment of all in the gang, the man flew from the saddle and fell to the ground. The moment was all that was needed.

"Inside!" the older boy ordered, pushing Mrs. Bradford through the door as Blake dashed in behind them.

"Here," Sarah called as she took another gun from one of the house servants and traded it for Tyler's empty. She passed it to another to reload.

The riders outside approached the front porch. "Yer all dead, Lady," one called.

Blake froze, not ready to shoot at another person.

"Ya gotta shoot em!" Tyler called. "Figure they's bears an'll kill ya if ya don't!"

Gunfire erupted from outside as wood splintered and glass shattered and the debri filled the air around the doorway. Using the door frame for cover, Tyler raised his gun and fired, knocking another from his horse. Blake followed his example, remembering all that Jackson had taught him and took down another. Bullets flew through the doorway and the windows.

"Git the children down!" Celia shouted. And the others in the hall suddenly reacted and took the younger children into the kitchen.

"Round back!" a killer shouted. The riders began to divide and some rode toward the back porch.

The boys took up another loaded rifle each and positioned themselves to fire on the enemy. The men outside fired on the house in unison. Each of the boys took advantage of a brief pause and picked a target, firing in short order and knocking down another of the attackers. Another blast from outside and there were screams from those inside.

"Sammy's hit," Celia cried.

"Lock the back door!" Charlotte ordered.

Tyler stumbled back against the wall. "I'm hit," he said. "I cain't lift ma arm."

There was a sudden roar of voices from outside. Daniel had arrived with the field hands and they were swarming around the buildings to get closer to the riders and pull them down with hay forks and shovels and bare hands. Jackson and his son ran for the guns they had been using to hunt with Blake. The killers were distracted by the dozens who were attacking them on foot, while the father and son slipped around to positions where they could cover the back porch. Men who were trying to break in the back door found themselves falling to the very people they were proposing to free.

Inside the front hall, the attack had been broken by the arrival of the field hands and attention was being given to the wounded. Sammy wasn't shot. He had tripped and fallen, hitting his head against the wall causing a very bloody scalp wound. Tyler had been grazed in his right forearm, but no serious damage was done. The house had been their protection and they had been lucky.

Quiet settled about the yard as the remaining attackers gave up to the overwhelming numbers arriving from the fields. Of the thirty who had ridden in with guns blazing, six were dead and another dozen were wounded, some critically.

A dust cloud could be seen coming up the pike from the south. But there was no sound.

"Git ready," Daniel ordered. "There may be more."

All took cover within and behind the nearest buildings. They waited.

There appeared another group of riders accompanied by a carriage. It was Bristol, come for Tyler, but with many riders alongside and behind the carriage.

"It's okay," Tyler announced as he recognized the carriage. "It's Bristol."

The riders approached the battleground. Jason Chase, Tyler's father, was with them. He explained, "Bristol saw the riders' cloud a dust far ahead a him on the road. He sensed trouble an came back fer he'p. Mr. Parker told us ta arm ourselves an hurry 'long, jest in case. I'm glad Bristol's instincts were good. We'll take care a these fellas and he'p ta clean up."

"Pa!" Tyler called from the porch as he hobbled down the steps. "Yer late. We took care a them." The boy was proud of their defense of the plantation, yet very happy to see his pa.

"Yer wounded," Jason observed.

"Jest a scratch. Sammy's much worse and he weren't even shot."

The abolitionists were rounded up and locked in a shed. Their wounded were put in with them for them to tend. The dead were loaded onto a wagon to be taken on to Shelby for burial. Their guns and ammunition were gathered up and put in the house in the library to be sorted out later and kept for future emergencies. Daniel gave the field hands the rest of the day off so attention could be given to clean up and repair around the house. Celia set up on the back porch and took care of the wounded from the house. Two more of the house staff had been hit by flying debri and suffered gashes to face and arms. Some of the field hands had been shot while trying to pull down the raiders.

Jason gathered his son's things from the house. Celia bandaged Tyler's arm and the boy allowed Blake to help him climb aboard the carriage.

"Daniel, if ya folks need anythin, send word and Mr. Parker will let us he'p."

"Thanks. Safe journey, an take good care a thet boy. Hope he'll be back agin an we kin avoid more danger." Daniel approached the carriage. "It's a fine thin ya did here, boy. I'm truly very proud a ya." He offered his hand and Tyler accepted with a sense of pride and honor.

"I'm leavin half my riders ta take the prisoners an the wagon a dead to Shelby. Ya all take care a thins here," Jason announced.

The prisoners were taken from their holding place, tied together in a group, then led up the road toward Shelby. One of them was ordered to drive the wagon. All left, the carriage with father, his horse tied to the back, and son and outriders to the south, and the riders with their prisoners to the north.

The people of the plantation settled to the business of cleaning up and healing those who were hurt.

* * *

After the attack, Blake had no more hesitation about leaving for the war and getting his father's killer.

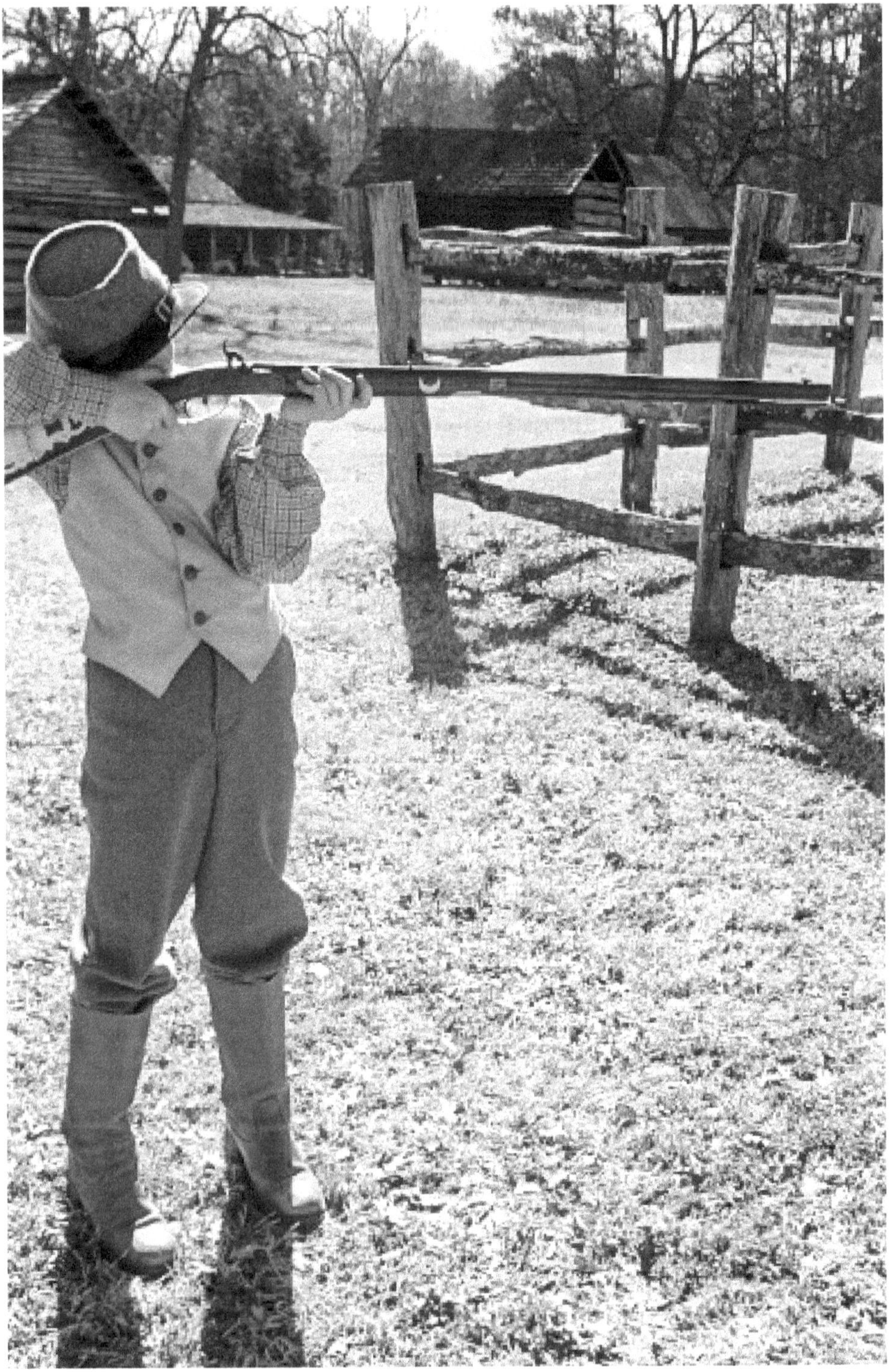

Chapter Three
By Way of Richmond

Throughout the summer Blake continued to hunt with James and improve his skills. Tyler visited again in early July and again toward the end of the month; and the two continued to play drum calls as they took time to hunt and fish together, and sometimes with James. Word of their defense of Bradford Plantation had gotten around and with it a respect that kept any more trouble far away. The plantation was never bothered again. The boy followed the progress of the Union Army as the large army that had been at Shiloh had moved south to Corinth. A smaller army was detached to operate in Tennessee and Kentucky. Two smaller Confederate armies moved into Tennessee and harassed the Federals by destroying railroad sections and burning bridges. One moved into Chatanooga and the other into Knoxville. They also raided smaller garrisons, capturing troops and supplies. There was no way to know if the Union troops that had fought Company J at Shiloh were with the army operating to the north or not. But Blake would take a chance that they might be because the Confederates to the north were closer and potentially easier to join. He learned that from time to time, Uncle Daniel would send a shipment of supplies from Shelby to the army by way of the railroad at Greeneville. A plan took shape.

On Thursday, August 8th, Blake was returning from a hunting trip with James when he saw an army horse tied at the back porch. The two had bagged a wild turkey each. James took his to his ma while Blake headed for the kitchen with his.

"See ya later tonight," he said waving James on his way. To himself he thought, "I wonder what this army officer wants."

"See ya then." The older boy was gone.

"Celia, I brought ya somethin," Blake announced as he passed through the kitchen and left the bird on the drain board.

"Ya ain't even cleaned it!" But the boy was already gone.

Passing the library door he saw the officer in conversation with his uncle near the desk by the window. He walked in and busied himself putting his gun and cartridge case in the gun cabinet, taking his time to overhear the conversation with his back to the men.

"Lieutenant," Daniel was saying, "I'll send this list a supplies ta Mr. Wilson in Shelby an he an Thompson will have the wagons loaded an ready ta leave by Saturday. You an yer troops kin pick 'em up then an take 'em ta the train at Greeneville. How will ya git them ta Gen'ral Bragg?"

"Not goin ta Bragg. Goin ta Gen'ral Kirby Smith's army in Knoxville. Thanks fer yer he'p."

"Yer welcome, Lieutenant. Since yer goin back ta Shelby, I'll put an auth'razation letter with this and ya kin give it ta Mr. Wilson when ya git back." Daniel sat down at the desk to write the letter.

The lieutenant turned and noticed the boy. "Thet's a nice lookin gun ya put in ther," he commented. "Kin I see it?"

Blake took his gun back out from the cabinet as the officer crossed the room to examine it. "It's an unusually fine rifle," he observed taking the offered weapon.

"My father gave it ta me on ma tenth birthday." His voice betrayed some emotion as well as a sense of pride.

"Is this yer pa?" he asked.

"His father was killed at Shiloh," Daniel stated, standing with the letter, ready for the officer. "I'm his uncle."

"Sorry, Boy." The lieutenant handed the gun back and turned to accept the letter. "I'll be goin now. An I'm truly sorry."

The officer tucked the letter into his uniform coat, picked up his hat from a side chair, and left the room through the kitchen through the back door.

"Did ya git enythin?" Daniel asked as Blake turned from putting his gun away.

"Left a turkey in the kitchen."

"You're doin good at yer huntin. We're eatin good fer it."

"Uncle Daniel," Blake asked. "Kin I ride Prince ta Shelby tamorra an git more cartridges? An I'd like ta stay over an watch the supply troops leave. I'd he'p with some chores fer ma keep."

"I'll talk ta yer mother tonight. Tell ya com mornin."

"Thanks. Gotta clean up fer supper."

He turned and left. The man listened as light footsteps crossed the hall and clicked up the steps.

* * *

The time had come. Blake would put his things together after supper, sneak his pack out to the barn after dark, and leave with the supply wagons on Saturday. Before going down for supper, he stuffed a change of clothes into his pack; a plate, cup, and utensils he had previously hidden in his wardrobe; added his drum sticks, strap, and hunting knife; then gathered together his bedroll, cartridge case, cap box, and an extra bag for food. There was a canteen in the barn. He would fill it at the well and hang it from the saddle. With the increasing heat and lack of rain in recent weeks, he would need all the water he could carry.

* * *

"I'm goin out ta see Jackson an James," Blake announced as he headed toward the kitchen and the back door. Passing the library, he slipped in to take his rifle and ammunition with him to the stables.

The boy stashed his gun and cartridge case in the hay beside Prince's stall, then slipped out the door toward Jackson's. The boy and his pa were seated on the front steps.

"What ya doin with yer gun?" James asked.

Blake didn't know he had been seen and had to think fast. "I'm goin ta Shelby tamorra ta git more cartridges fer practice an huntin." Then he added, "Uncle Daniel said I could stay over and watch the supply wagons leave fer the army." If they expected him to be gone, maybe no one would look for him until he was too far along his way.

"I fergot," he turned back, "need ta fill the canteen fer the trip. It sher is gittin hotter these days," he added as he went back into the stable and took it down from its peg. Walking to the well, he drew the water and filled the container, then returned it to the barn and hung it near Prince's stall. Returning to James and his pa, he settled on the steps with them.

"Be careful," Jackson advised. "If eny sees ya alone 'long the road thet's begrudged a last month, it could git dangerous."

"I hope ma gun 'll keep 'em from doin enythin."

"Git some extra caps an cartridges fer me too," James added. "I'm gitten low an hope we kin go huntin Saturday next."

"Sher will."

The three sat quietly watching the fireflies begin to flash in the heat of the night air as twilight crept in. As the black of night rose from the eastern horizon, the small sliver of the quarter moon became visible above the trees. The evening air was clear and the deepening darkness cast dim shadows about the yard.

"What was it like at night?" Blake asked.

"Some nights were quiet like this with noises of insects an sech. Jest an extra background noise from all the soldiers talking ta one 'nother." Jackson leaned back against the building as he gazed at the sky. "Others, it rained an we was sorely miserable."

"I 'member one night the bands was playin an the air was filled with music," James added. "There was one night when we was settin out by the train, waitin fer a bridge ta be fixed, thet the world was bright as day fer the moon was full. It were truly a beautiful sight."

"Ya wish ya was back?" the boy asked.

"No way," James responded.

"Only if the captain was still alive," Jackson added.

The twilight deepened and the night sounds of the crickets and tree toads filled the air. Jackson stood up and stretched, his shirt stuck to the sweat on his back.

"Mornin comes early and there's sleep a callin. Time fer bed."

"Night," the boys chorused.

Blake started across the yard as the father and son stepped into their quarters for the night. He entered the house and passed through to the parlor where he found his mother, working on some hand work, and uncle, reading a newspaper.

"Night, Mother." He kissed her on the cheek. "Night, Uncle Daniel." He turned toward the door.

"Night," they both answered.

In his room, Blake gathered his things for his journey and quietly descended the servants' stairs to the kitchen. He paused to cut a hunk of Sarah's bread and put it in his food bag. Then he crossed the yard, being careful that no one was out, entered the stable and added his gear to the place in the hay with his rifle. Taking the food bag and his hunting knife, Blake went to the smoke house and carefully cut off a large piece of smoked beef, wrapped it in a cloth, and placed it in the bag. Hanging the food bag from a peg in the rafters to keep varmints from it, he quietly returned to the house, to his room, and quietly went to bed.

* * *

The blanket roll was tied securely to the back of the saddle. The pack and bags were hung to the side of the saddle away from the view of those at the house. Prince was led to the door and tied just inside. The rifle and cartridge case were leaned against the door. Blake walked to the house to say good-bye.

The boy's uncle had seen him during the early part of the morning and told him his mother had given her permission, then had gone to the fields. The younger children were with Sarah in the kitchen with their hands fully involved in making cookies. Mother was busy at her desk in the library writing a letter to a friend.

Charlotte looked up as her son entered. "Ya be safe an take care a yerse'f." She turned her face up for a kiss. "See ya tamorra."

"I luv ya, Mother. See ya later." Passing through the kitchen he offered a quick, "Bye." And was gone.

Blake felt good. No one would come out and no one would see that he had packed all he was taking. Picking up the rifle and throwing the cartridge strap over his shoulder, Blake mounted Prince and rode toward the lane and the pike to Shelby.

"Bye, Blake!" It was Sammy, climbing the back steps with an arm full of firewood.

"Bye," Blake waved, hoping the houseboy wouldn't notice all he had packed.

Sammy turned his attention to getting up the steps without tripping and Blake guided Prince out onto the pike and north toward Shelby.

* * *

Bradford General Store and Freight had grown into a very large and profitable business. The North Carolina Railroad spur tied back to the main line all the way to Richmond. Mountains of supplies had accumulated in the yard behind the main buildings and had to be shipped by wagon to connect to the armies in the west. The main connection was by wagon to Greeneville where the Virginia and Tennessee Railroad could move shipments to western railroads and destinations.

As Blake approached the store, a plan formed in his mind. The family didn't expect him back until the next day, but Justin Wilson and the folks at the store didn't know that. He tied Prince at the post in front and went inside.

"Hey, Blake," Justin greeted. "What brings ya here this day?"

"I bin doin a lot a huntin and need lots more cartridges." The boy approached the counter. He leaned his rifle against the side and stood for a moment gazing at all the activity of customers and work staff.

"How much ya need?"

"I'd guess about two hundred cartridges and three hundred caps."

"How ya goin ta carry it?"

"I got Prince outside."

"I'll pack a pair a saddle bags fer ya." Justin turned to one of the clerks. "Danny, go inta the store room an fetch a set a saddle bags, then put a box a cartridges in each pouch an three tins a caps in one."

"Yes, Sir. Git right on it."

"Enythin else?"

"Ya got somthin fer rain an wet weather?" Blake remembered what James and his pa had said about stormy weather so much. It would be good if he had something to help stay dry. "I need a large canteen, too. It's really hot these days. An do ya have a hav'sack? It would come in handy ta carry thins when I'm huntin."

"Danny, find the boy a gum blanket, one with a hole like a poncho, he kin wear, and check fer the largest canteen we have, an don't fergit a hav'sack." Justin reached in a drawer for a ledger book. "Put this in the book fer yer uncle?"

"Yes, Sir. I best be headin back fer it gits too late."

"Here's yer supplies." Danny laid the saddle bags and canteen across his shoulder and handed him the gum blanket and haversack.

"Thanks. See ya all later." He waved and turned to leave.

Once outside, Blake explored to find out where the soldiers were camped and how far progress was at getting the wagons loaded. He found the wagons in the back storage yard near the piles of supplies, still in the process of being loaded.

"Sergeant, where does this go," one of the workmen asked.

"Thet goes in the fourth wagon with the other food supplies."

"I think we're almost finished, Sir," another of the workmen, carrying an inventory order observed.

"Okay," the sergeant instructed. "We have many days ahead a us. So when ya've finished, put the canvass covers back over the wagons ta he'p pratect the loads."

Blake put his new supplies across in front of Prince's saddle, hanging the canteen and haversack on the saddle horn, and climbed up. He would be back after he found the soldiers' camp. It didn't take long. The camp was set on the yard in front of the schoolhouse. Passing by, he paused to fill his new canteen at the schoolhouse water pump. Next, he rode over to the stable to talk to Homer Riley about leaving Prince for the night. His mother had said he could stay over and watch the supply train leave the next day.

"When yer ready, bring Prince and put his saddle an bridle on the wooden horse beside his stall. Use the stall in the back. I'll feed and water him." Homer led the boy to the stall he had selected.

"Thanks, Homer. I'll bring him back as soon's I've unloaded." Blake rode back towards the supply wagons.

By the time he returned, the wagons had been loaded and the canvass tops had been secured in place. He picked the fourth wagon; it had food. Checking inside, there was no place to hide, so he moved on. The fifth wagon had blankets and canvass supplies. It was better. Tying Prince to the back side of the wagon, away from the general view of the yard, Blake carefully lifted the side of the canvass and shifted the load to create a pocket he could hide in. It would be a very hot trip. He hoped he could keep hidden in spite of the heat, and was glad for the second canteen. Then he unloaded his pack, bags, saddle bags, canteens, and blanket roll and put them in the open space. He would take Prince back to the stable, then change into his uniform pants, crawl into the empty space, and pull canvass and blankets over top to keep him hidden, but arranged to let in as much air as possible. Here he would stay for the ride to Greeneville. At night he would sneak out to use the trees, get some fresh air, and refill his canteens. During the day he would stay hidden where he had food and the canteens of water.

* * *

The supply train had left Shelby around mid morning on Saturday. At Greeneville, Blake waited for the soldiers to leave the wagons and get something to eat, then he quietly moved his gear, filled the empty space with canvass and blankets, and climbed out of the wagon. He then took his gear into the freight depot where he could repack it so it could be carried on his back. The blankets were re-rolled into the gum blanket to be tied over the top of his pack. The extra cartridges were transferred into his pack and the saddle bags were abandoned. He put on his drum strap and drum stick case, stuffed the forage cap in his pack, and wore his own hat. Having brought all the money he had from his bedroom, a little over $20.00, he put a dollar in his pockets and the rest in the bottom of his pack. He was ready.

Early the next morning, Blake hefted his pack onto his back; slipped the haversack over his shoulder; put on his cartridge box, cap box, and canteens; stuck his hat on his head, his hair already plastered to his forehead from the heat; picked up his rifle; and walked into the station building.

"I need a ticket fer Knoxville," he announced to the stationmaster as he placed his dollar on the counter. The astonished agent stared at the boy, too surprised to speak, then looked at the money.

"Thet ain't gonna git ya there," the man stated after he got over the surprise.

"But I'm the new drummer fer the Tennessee 19th fer Tyler Chase who was wounded at Shiloh. I'm on the way ta enlist."

"Whar's yer drum?"

"Ain't reg'lation. Had ta leave it ta home."

"What's yer name, Boy?" a new voice asked from behind.

"Bradford James, Sir." The voice sounded familiar.

"Give him his money back an give him his ticket," the voice continued. "He's with the supply train an I'm the officer in charge." To the boy, he ordered, "Private Bradford James, wait outside."

"Yes, Sir." Blake turned and saw the lieutenant standing there. He wasn't very happy. The boy saluted and did as he was told.

* * *

"What the Sam Hill ya think yer doin, Bradford James?" the lieutenant asked once they were outside of earshot from anyone.

"I'm goin ta the war ta do ma duty an kill yanks," he stated firmly, standing tall.

"I know yer pa were kilt at Shiloh, but ya ain't old 'nough ta be in the army."

"I'm old enough ta be a drummer." He looked the officer square in the face.

"Yer twelve?"

"Yes, Sir," he replied without hesitation.

"Yer family know yer here?"

"No, Sir."

The lieutenant took the boy by the shoulder and drew him to the edge of the platform. "Sit down," he instructed.

Blake sat on the edge of the floorboards, hanging his feet over the side. The officer descended the steps, walked to his side, and leaned against the edge.

"We do have a problem," he began. "Yer name may be Bradford, but it's not Bradford James. How clever. I'm Lieutenant Warren, Anthony Warren, with the 2nd Tennessee Volunteer Infantry under Brigadeer General Cleburne. I have been detached with this company to take this supply train to General Kirby Smith's army at Knoxville." He paused, struck by a question. "How did ya git here enyway?"

"I rode in one a yer wagons." Blake slipped his pack off to rest on the floor planking and get some air on his wet shirt.

"There's no way ya could spend five days in a wagon and not need ta git out nor have nothing ta eat."

"I went out at night and had ma own provisions. Ate light so's not ta need ta go out much." Nervous at first, his voice began to settle to more calm.

"We do have a problem, Bradford. We're too fer away ta send ya back." The man stood away from the wooden platform and began to pace. "I'll take ya with us an try ta look afta ya. We git on the train an find a drummer 'long the way an ya prove yer a drummer, an I'll find ya a company as needs a drummer. 'Member, ya stay close by an folla any orders as I see needin fer yer best safety." The lieutenant turned and faced the boy. "If this Tyler you mentioned is real, then I'm sure he's told you this is a very dangerous thing yer doin."

"He's real, all right. He was with ma father and was wounded. He lost his foot an cain't go back. I know the dangers."

A sergeant approached the two.

"We're loaded, Lieutenant. The supplies ar in the box cars at the front a the train."

"Thank ya, Sergeant. Git the troops on board the fust coach." Pulling Blake off the platform he continued, "Sergeant Harris, this is Bradford James. He'll be goin with us until he finds his company and enlists."

"Yes, Sir."

"Now let's git ever'one on board." To Blake he added, "Fer yer information, the 19th Tennessee is in Mississippi an ya'll be assigned ta a company in the 2nd Tennessee."

* * *

The train traveled southwest on the Virginia & Tennessee Railroad to Knoxville. Along the way it picked up a company of new recruits headed for Chatanooga, and Blake got his chance to prove he was a drummer. The lieutenant and his company were impressed. So were the new recruits.

On Monday, August 18th, the supply train arrived at Knoxville, only to find that General Kirby Smith had left the previous Wednesday on assignment to enter Kentucky to support General Bragg's army, invading Kentucky hoping to arouse the supporters of the Confederacy to swell the ranks of the army and secure its secession into the Confederacy. The supplies and troops were unloaded from the rail cars onto a new train of wagons to head north over the Cumberland Mountains to join Smith's army in Kentucky. Meanwhile, Bragg's army remained in Chattanooga.

The supply train followed Smith, crossing through the Cumberland Mountains by way of Big Creek Gap, located several miles southwest of the Cumberland Gap, which was garrisoned with a Union force of 8,000 men. Ten days later, the supplies were delivered to Smith's army and Lieutenant Warren and his company were back with their 2nd Tennessee in General Hill's Brigade of General Cleburne's Division of General Kirby Smith's army.

As the wagons approached London, Kentucky, finally leaving the poor barren regions of southeastern Kentucky and approaching the rich blue grass region of good farm land, the morning temperatures were heading toward the 90's and the clouds of silty dust rose around the wagons and the company of soldiers bringing them to the army. Animals and men alike were coated with dust as it clung to their sweat, covered wagon canvass, and matted in their hair. The wagons were a welcome site to the supply train having had great difficulty in acquiring provisions along the way throughout the campaign so far.

Lieutenant Warren reported to his captain, Captain Jonathan Wilson, returning his small detachment of troops to bring the compliment back to its strength of thirty-two soldiers and officers. The returning troops settled in to the encampment of troops, bivouacked in the fields north of London with the rest of the brigade, along side the Old State Road. More than three thousand troops in Cleburne's division were encamped in the area, in advance of the rest of General Kirby Smith's army.

Blake shared a cooking fire with privates Todd Johnson and Aidan Larken. The lieutenant had made the assignment to give him time to find a more permanent assignment. The three had just finished cleaning up from dinner when the lieutenant approached their fire. He squatted in front of the boy.

"Bradford," he began, "Captain Wilson informs me that our drummer took sick back in Knoxville an was left behind. I've been instructed ta muster ya inta the company an Sergeant Harris has added ya to the company roster. The drum is somewhar in the supply wagons, so fer now yer bein assigned curier duty ta Colonel Butler, ar regimental commander. Kin ya ride?"

"Yes, Sir. Bin riden as fer back as I kin 'member." The boy stood up to talk to the officer. The lieutenant stood up as well. "When da I report an whar?"

"Come mornin we'll git ya a horse an take ya ta the colonel. Come fust light, ya pack up an git somethin ta eat." The officer turned and left.

"Spread yer blankets here b'side ar's," Todd offered.

"Yer lucky," Aidan added. "They ain't found ya a jacket yet an thet's a blessin in this heat."

"Ain't complainin," the boy remarked as he settled on top of his blankets. It was way too hot to climb under.

As each settled in and the air hummed with the quiet conversations of a thousand soldiers, drummers throughout the brigade sounded taps. A myriad of flickering candle lanterns began to wink out and the blackness of the heavens was flooded with a carpet of twinkling lights. The army slept.

* * *

Friday dawned hot and dry as the sounds of reveille brought life into the waking camps. Aidan was showing the boy how to dunk his hardtack in a cup of coffee to make it soft enough to eat, when Sergeant Harris arrived. The twenty-four-year-old looked older than his years having grown a scraggly beard which matched the brown of his long, untrimmed hair. He was carrying something.

"One a the boys found this among some things ar drummer left behind. It might be a bit big, but thet's better 'an bein too tight." He handed a jacket to Blake. "Can't have ya out a uniform an ridin fer the colonel. I've sent Campbell ta git ya a horse. Soon's he's back, I'll take ya to the colonel. Git yer gear packed." The boy slipped the jacket over his sweat-soak shirt and vest. He had already traded his hat for the grey kepi, having stuffed the hat into the bottom of his pack for safe keeping.

The man left.

"Hey, Bradford." It was Corporal Elias Campbell, leading a well groomed grey toward him. "This here mare's well bred and well trained. She's also experienced, having been in combat at Shiloh. The corporal who assigned her to ya said as the staff officer who rode her at Shiloh was kilt when Colonel Bate, our regimental commander then, was wounded. She should be good fer ya." He brought the horse to the boy and held her as he suggested, "Roll yer bedroll an gum blanket an tie it behind the saddle. Less weight on yer back." Blake did as he was told. "Yer not gonna be able to hold yer gun an do yer job. I'll git ya a piece a rawhide ta tie ta it so's ya kin hang it on yer back like a canteen."

Sergeant Harris returned on horseback as Blake finished settling his gear in order, and mounted the grey.

"Ready?"

"Yes, Sir."

"Let's ride."

As the two rode off to the regimental staff gathering along-side the Old State Road, the drums began their roll and the regiments of Cleyburne's division were assembled in order with their brigade commanders, preparing to continue the march toward Lexington. Sergeant Harris introduce Bradford James to the colonel, then left him and returned to the company.

The couriers from the various regiments were sent to General Cleburne's staff to pick up orders for the day. Blake learned that there was a unit of cavalry under Colonel Scott about five miles ahead on the road and that the division was to be the advance guard for the army. As such, they would be moving up the road first. The boy returned with his instructions for the colonel.

The 2nd Tennessee moved out first as the remaining three regiments of Colonel Hill's brigade fell in behind and Colonel Preston Smith followed with his brigade. Cleburne's division was on the move with more than three thousand men.

Great clouds of dust rose up from the parched earth and enveloped the army. The temperature rose into the 90's. The men suffered in the heat as their woolen uniforms became soaked with their sweat and coated with the dust that clung to their hair, parched lips, and the hairs of their nostrils. Slowly the mass moved north. The sun rose to its zenith then dropped toward the western horizon as the day progressed and the soldiers suffered. Crossing the branches of the Rockcastle River, the army passed through a gap in the hills toward an elevation known as Big Hill.

Around 2 o'clock in the afternoon sounds of gunfire drifted in from the north. It seemed to dissipate. The sounds of cannon roared to the front at about 5 PM. Then quiet and a cavalry officer came riding through to meet with General Cleburne. Orders flew as riders rushed back and forth between command and unit commanders. The division was formed up in line of battle, facing the direction of the enemy. The men of the front brigade, which included the 2nd Tennessee, were ordered to stand to arms and be ready to move at a moment's notice. By the time this had been accomplished, it was after dark. The 2nd was placed beside the pike and the remaining three regiments in line to the right. The soldiers were dismissed to set camp and light their fires.

In short order firing and yelling were heard to the front and cavalry soldiers, sick men, baggage wagons, and servants leading horses began charging through the camp closely followed by Federal cavalry. The lines were quickly reformed and the road left open for the retreating troops.

Blake was riding alongside the colonel.

"Colonel, what the heck is going on?" Blake asked Colonel Butler.

Colonel Butler answered roughly, "Son, you are in a war."

Blake looked out into the battlefield. "Wait, how did I get in the…" He paused. A bullet flew overhead.

Two companies from the 48th Tennessee, just beside the 2nd, fired on the enemy and they stopped. One regiment of Federal cavalry dismounted and again advanced. It was dark, just a sliver of a moon, and the enemy couldn't see the lines of Confederate soldiers, the action having brought them some 300 yards from their campfires. There was a deafening roar as the enemy kept up a continuous fire on the campfires. A few sharpshooters were pushed forward and the Federal soldiers stopped their advance and refused commands to move up. The explosion of riflery mixed with the shouts of orders laced with curses and threats from enemy officers pressed on the boy's nerves. The action was short-lived as the Federals gave way and retreated in confusion, leaving behind prisoners, guns, and horses.

The men of the brigade settled for the night without any supper and slept in line of battle. Their casualties were 1 man wounded.

* * *

Saturday morning dawned another hot and dry day. At daylight, a company of cavalry was sent forward to find the enemy. Hill's brigade began to move along with a battery of artillery, followed by a quarter mile by Colonel Preston Smith's brigade, also with a battery of artillery. Blake soon found himself in a line of battle on the right side of the road within a few hundred yards of the enemy. A brief explosion of gunfire filled the air as the two armies engaged for a short time. The boy heard the whistle of bullets as they passed through the air near him, and suddenly felt afraid. Very shortly, the enemy skirmishers fell back to their main army. A battery of artillery was placed in front of the Confederate line near its center. Blake suddenly felt the vibration of air all about him and the pressure of the concussion as the artillery and musketry opened against the enemy and the enemy fired back. The air filled with the screams of agony, the shouts of orders, the explosion of artillery, the roaring clatter of musket fire, and the life blood of wounded and dying soldiers. Colonel Butler scribbled some notes and handed them to the boy to take to Hill. As Blake turned his horse he heard the swarm of bullets, felt the pull on his clothing as some passed through, and heard a nearby thump. Glancing in the direction of the last noise as he pulled away toward Hill, he saw Butler lean forward in his saddle, then slip to the ground as several of his aides rushed to his side. Men were falling all along the line as Blake rode. The engagement lasted for two fear-filled hours. But reflex action took hold and the boy soon forgot his fear, being too busy to dwell upon it. A second battery opened from the lines of the brigade and the compression of the conflict became more intense. A surge of motion of masses of men began to sweep across the landscape as enemy troops began to push along the Confederate right and the regiments of Smith's brigade located behind the front began to shift toward the right to meet the enemy and push them back. As the conflict roared on, Blake saw thousands more troops arrive and pour into position against the enemy along the left side of the action. Around one o'clock, he heard heavy fighting about one half mile to the west and witnessed Yankees to his front and left retreating in poor order. The Federal line broke and began to fall back toward Richmond. The boy carried instructions that the brigade would strike the center of the new Federal position, setting up some two miles further north. General Cleburne had been wounded and Colonel Preston Smith was in command. Blake found Captain Charles P. Moore was in temporary command of the regiment.

The concussion of battle faded as the Union line retreated north, up the Richmond Pike toward the cemetery, and the temperature soared into the upper 90's.

A new Federal position was established on a commanding ridge with its left on a stone wall in the cemetery and its right protected by a wooded thicket. The men of Cleburne's command were tired. They had fought all day without water. Blake watched from Colonel Smith's command as the men in the frontal attack scrambled up the slope of the ridge and poured over the stone wall. The cheering troops engaged the Federals in fierce hand to hand combat among the tombstones of the cemetery. More troops smashed into the wooded thicket. The Federal troops got off about three rounds of musket fire, then panicked, turned, and fled. They raced back through the town and onto the Lexington Road. This time Colonel Scott's cavalry met them from the back side of the town, having been sent around to the back of the enemy earlier in the day.

It was over.

General Kirby Smith had lost 78 killed, 372 wounded, and 1 missing. The Union Army had lost 206 killed, 844 wounded, 4303 captured. Blake felt proud to have been a part of it. He learned later that Colonel Butler had been killed during the action.

* * *

It was nearing seven o'clock in the evening as the battle came to a close. Blake returned to his company as the regiments started back to their camps. The men were exhausted, miserable from the heat, hungry, and thirsty. As they headed south across the battlefield they observed the wreckage of war. The dead lay about the fields along with dead horses, broken artillery, scattered equipment and personal gear. The air was filled with the moans and cries of the wounded. It was filled, too, with the stench of death as the heat of the high 90's hastened the decay of the dead, and the stench of sweat-soaked wool on the living whose clothing clung to their bodies, saturated in their own perspiration and heated by the bodies within and the air temperatures without. They walked in silence, stunned by what they had experienced and the scene of destruction that surrounded them and the bloody ground beneath their feet.

"Bradford." It was young Todd Johnson. "Ya okay?"

The boy walked silently beside his comrade, leading his horse, his rifle still slung over his shoulder and hanging on his wet back. "I guess," he responded checking the holes in his uniform. "I hate war," he whispered. "I jest left the colonel when he was kilt. My friend, Tyler, was with my father when he was kilt. He saw the face of the soldier thet did it. Taday ya couldn't see them. They was too fer away." He swept the scene with his hand. "All 'bout these wounded are hurtin and cryin an I don't know what ta do fer em." His voice was on the edge of breaking as tears slipped down his cheeks.

"Hey, Soldier," a soft voice called from nearby. "Help me."

Todd stopped, startled by the voice. Searching for the voice, he found a young Union soldier, about his own age, lying along the side of the pike. He walked over and knelt in the blood-soaked mud beside him.

"What's yer name?" he asked.

"Roger, Roger Stanley."

"How old ar ya, Roger?"

"Sixteen."

"How bad ya hurt?"

"I'm done for." He opened his shirt. "A shell fragment went right through." The wound under his shirt was a ragged hole through his lower ribs, soaked red with blood and gore leaking from the boy's body, saturating his clothes and puddling on the ground.

The boys covered their noses. "The stink is fearsome," Blake stated.

He knelt beside Todd and handed him his canteen as the older youth closed the bloody shirt and covered the wound. "Water?" Todd offered.

Roger took the canteen and drank. "Thanks." He shuddered in pain and clenched his fists.

Others in the company paused to watch. Captain Wilson walked over. "There's hospitals in most a these barns," he suggested.

"Too late fer this one," Todd stated. "I'll stay here a while if it's okay, Sir."

"Kin I?" Blake asked.

"Yes, but come straight back soon's yer done."

"Yes, Sir," Blake responded.

The rest of the company continued on their way. Blake and Todd remained with the dying soldier. Little was said. The two sat in silence, their eyes on the youth lying on the ground.

"Hold me," Roger begged, his voice fading.

Todd gathered him into his lap and leaned over to embrace him. He felt the body quiver as if catching a chill. Blake watched, crying within. *This wasn't the enemy? He's jest a kid! Tyler said he saw the soldier who killed his father. He said he was jest a kid, too.*

The body stilled. Todd felt the warmth fade from the face as he caressed the skin and laid him back down. Tears slid down his face and dripped from his cheeks. He stood up. "Let's go," he said.

"We kin ride ma horse," Blake offered.

Todd climbed on first, then reached down and pulled his younger companion up and helped him slip on behind.

The two started back toward the army's camps, about five miles south of the town.

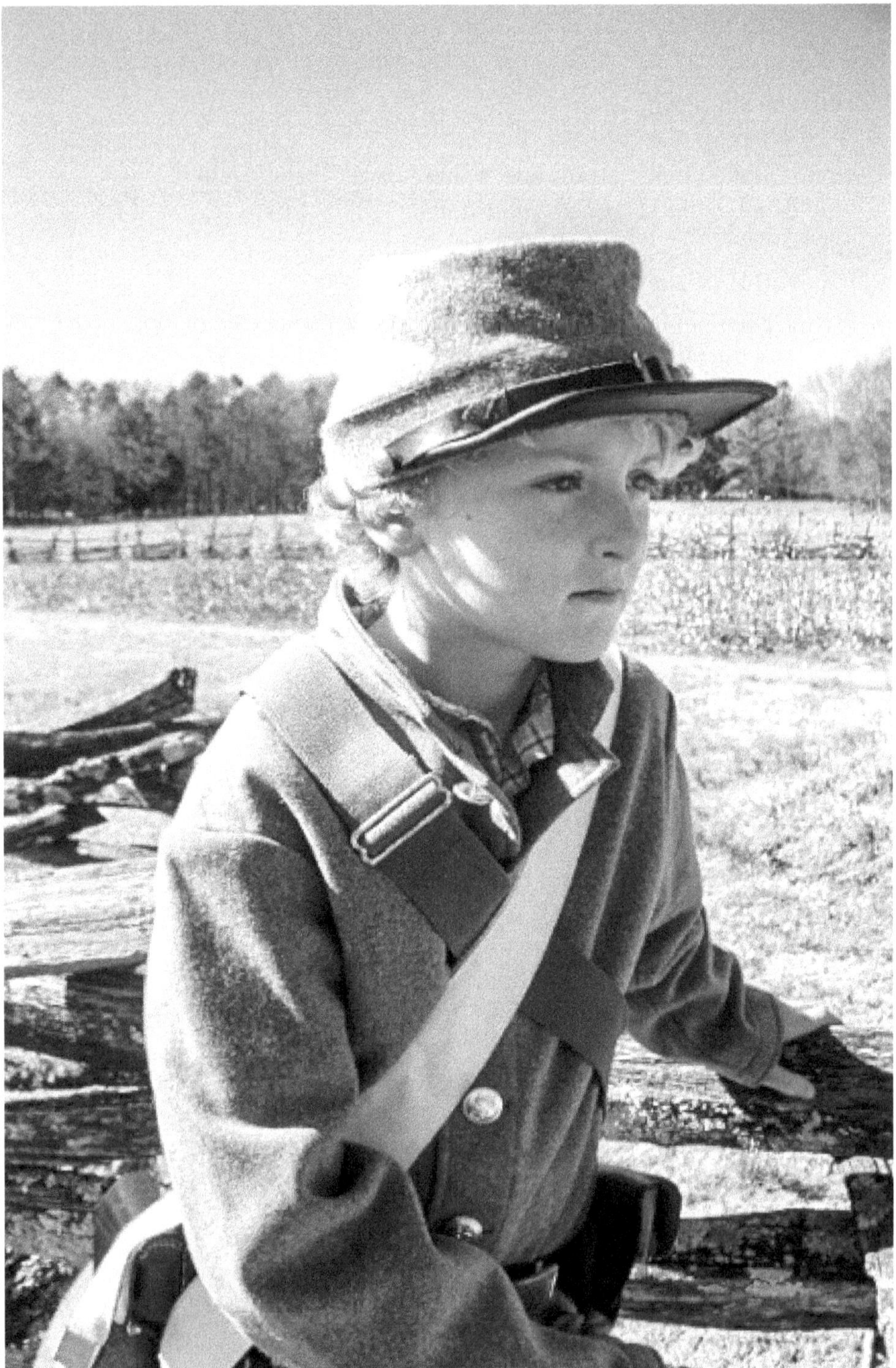

Chapter Four
Union Army at Perryville

"Brandon, time fer reveille." The boy opened his eyes and found Sergeant Harris standing by his bedroll. "Found this in the supply wagon." He presented Blake with a field drum. "Wake the camp."

The army had rested a day and many who had marched barefoot from Knoxville, received shoes from the captured Union supply wagons. The men of the 4th Arkansas finally traded their flintlocks for captured Springfield rifles. Spirits were high, and so were the temperatures in the continuing drought which had parched the landscape for many weeks. Monday, September 1st would be a day for travel.

Rubbing the sleep from his eyes, Blake pulled on his boots, slipped on his jacket, found his strap and sticks, then stood to accept the drum. Attaching it to the clip on the strap, he took his sticks from their case and beat reveille.

"Ar boy has his job," Todd announced as he sat up on his blankets, then got to his feet. "Som'ne git the fire up an some coffee brewin."

All along the line of waking men and boys, bedrolls were rolled up and tied to their packs and fires were stirred up for coffee and hardtack.

"Cain't wait til we git inta the Union supply train an git somthin more then hardtack ta eat," Aidan said as he rolled his blankets and dug out his tin cup.

The men had barely had time to eat before the sergeant was back. "Sound assembly, Brandon," he ordered.

The company was assembled and the captain explained the orders for the day. "We break camp and march north ta Lexington, 'bout twenty-five miles. There we'll make a reg'lar camp an stay while the gen'ral decides what's next. Be ready ta move in a half hour." He turned and left.

Lieutenant Warren instructed, "Sergeant, dismiss the men and be sure they're packed ta go."

The men were dismissed and finished packing their gear for the march north.

"What happens ta all thet's out on the fields?" Blake asked.

Aidan explained, "There's litter brigades from various companies is assigned to pick up the wounded an git them ta the hospitals an others ta bury the dead. They'll probably dig a big hole up by the cemetery an put ever'one in. There'll be scavengers on the battlefield taking keepsakes from the wreckage an some as'll rob the dead of anythin of value. The people 'round here'll git thins cleaned up." The seventeen-year-old finished packing, then stood and put his pack on his back, ready to move on.

Sergeant Harris approached Blake. "Time to go."

The boy struck the long roll and the soldiers gathered. A rider passed by ordering, "Colors and musicians to the front," and moved on.

The large square Confederate battle flag along with the regimental banner and all company musicians moved to the front of the regiment. The companies lined up in order of march. All up and down the ranks of the brigade orders rang out and soldiers assumed their places. Troops fell into rank, four abreast, and chaos took on order. Officers rode up and down the lines giving instructions. Finally all was ready. The brigade command staff was in front of the colors and each regimental command staff was in front of its regiment.

On instructions from the general, one of the staff officers turned to the drum major, a musician in his early twenties carrying a fancy staff, and gave the command, "Beat, off!"

The collective drummers struck the march and the collective fifers struck the melody. The army began to move. It was another day of dry heat and the clouds of dust rose quickly and enveloped the men and horses and wagons and batteries of artillery.

* * *

Along the way, soldiers were provisioned from the Union supply wagons. Spirits were high among the three divisions of Kirby Smith's army. On Thursday the 4th they entered Lexington.

"Listen ta thet crowd," Corporal Alexander Fox exclaimed. "They are so full of joy!"

"Don't it feel good," William Kramer added.

"It really feels good as we're eatin better," Todd put in. "But I wish this infernal heat would quit. I'm tired a walkin in soakin wet clothes an breathin dust in ma lungs."

"When's Brandon git back," Aidan asked as the sergeant passed by to the side of the company.

"When we set camp," the sergeant replied.

They could hear the musicians. Their tunes had filled the air throughout the day and given a constant cadence for the march, which as the day went on had become more of a rhythmic walk. Now all about them the crowds cheered in a joyous frenzy.

"Look sharp," Harris instructed. "Pick up the beat and git in step with the cadence."

Conversation quieted as the soldiers picked up their feet in time with the music and with it a feeling of pride. To the people of Lexington they were an impressive sight.

* * *

A thousand cook fires crackled throughout the countryside. General Kirby Smith had settled his army in camp to await further developments from General Bragg who commanded the other Confederate Army on the move to the west. Upon arrival at Lexington, the army had taken a small Union garrison and all the supplies held therein. Finally his army could receive food issues as well as clothing and equipment that was sorely needed.

"Aidan," Blake smiled, "we finally got some real food, salt beef, some potatoes, flour ta make bread, an coffee thet tastes like coffee."

"Yeh," Aidan agreed, "ya think the potatoes ar done yet?"

"Is the mud hard like clay?" Todd asked.

Aidan reached into the hot coals with a stick and tapped at the mud lumps. "Hard as rock," he observed.

"Then roll em out," Todd instructed.

The clay balls were rolled from the fire and gathered in a pile. The meat sizzled on the tin plates as each carefully balanced his on the fire wood pieces. Bread dough had been mixed on another plate and each took a shaved stick after setting aside his plate of meat and rolled a piece of dough to wrap on the stick. Holding the stick over the fire, each cooked his bread until it was dark brown, nearly black, then tested it for softness. Not soft? It was done.

"Ah, food," Todd sighed.

They ate in silence, savoring every bite. Throughout the camp soldiers were enjoying the bounty of the Union supply train, not just the food, but shoes and clothing and replacement equipment as well. When all had eaten, they wiped down their plates and utensils with grass and dirt, then rinsed them off with some water from their canteens. All was set aside as they poured their cups of coffee and settled about the fire.

Sergeant Harris came by. "You boys git settled in okay?" he asked. "We's gonna be here a while."

"Coffee?" Blake offered reaching for the coffee pot. Harris reached out his cup as the boy poured.

"What's next, Sergeant?" Aidan asked.

Standing by the fire and sipping on his coffee, the sergeant replied. "We've bin here waitin on Bragg. Hear he's at Glasgow, far west a here. Thanks fer the coffee. Gotta move on. Back later fer taps."

The evening drifted to twilight then toward dark as the sun slipped to the horizon and darkness crept in out of the east. The drummers struck taps throughout the camps and the murmurs of conversation dwindled to be replaced by the loudness of the insects in the warmth of the continuing drought.

* * *

As September drifted by, Smith's army remained at Lexington and Bragg's army moved slowly northeasterly in that general direction. On the 17th, Bragg had his first victory of the campaign when he captured the Union garrison at Munfordsville and all its supplies. On the 20th, he left there to Bardstown where he planned to meet with General Kirby Smith. The general did not meet him there and he had to go to Lexington to meet with Smith. As September neared its end, Cleburne's division was recalled to Bragg's army from which it had been borrowed back in August. Once more Blake was on the move as the 2nd and all the rest in the division marched to Shelbyville, to the west of Lexington, just beyond the state capital at Frankfort. On October 2nd, a large Union force took Shelbyville, driving the division toward Frankford and eventual reunion with its original corps commander, Major General William Hardee. General Buell's Union Army was on the move and General Bragg began sending his divisions and brigades to the southeast with General Hardee headed toward Harrodsburg, northeast of Perryville. The march was hard with high temperatures and the continuing drought and the men increasingly desperate for water.

It was Tuesday afternoon, the 7th of October, as Hardee's divisions bivouacked to the north of Perryville. Provisions had dwindled to little more than hard biscuits and coffee. Soldiers spread their blankets and set their fires.

Corporal Alexander Fox wandered by with some sticks of firewood he had gathered along the way. "Ya hear what Gen'ral Bragg was doin last weekend while we're all marchin the countryside?"

"I heard he weren't with us," Blake acknowledged.

"Thet's right," Alex continued. "He was back at Frankfort with some a his army havin a real fancy time makin some guy gov'nor. The new gov'nor made his speech an then the Union Army arrived an they all skedaddled. He ain't gov'nor no more."

"An I heard there's bin some fightin 'round here'bouts," William Cramer, who had wandered by with the corporal, added. "There could be a big fight shapin up."

Todd came wandering back with some scraps of wood for the fire. "Bradford, I passed the sergeant on the way an he says as the capt'n wants ta see ya." He dropped the wood beside the fire site.

"We'll see ya later," Alex said as he and William left to their own fire.

Blake stood from where he was breaking up wood for the fire. "Guess I'll see what the captain wants." He left towards the captain's bivouac site.

As he walked the line of fire sites with the bedding laid out by each soldier he marveled at the vastness of the scene. There were no tents, only acres upon acres of thousands of men spread out across the parched landscape. The Chaplin River was nearby, but it was mostly a dry bed with scattered puddles. Soldiers with canteens and coffee pots wandered in search of puddles deep enough to provide some water.

Ahead was the captain, conferring with his officers. Blake paused to wait his turn.

"Private James," Captain Wilson called, "come here please." As Blake approached the other officers remained. "I have an uneasy feeling about tomorrow and my officers concur." Blake, too, felt an uneasiness. "We think there might be some very serious fightin. It's only mid-afternoon, an there's already been a number of skirmishes in the area. With somethin this big we'll need a number of couriers an ya've done courier b'fer. Lieutenant Warren 'll see ta the details an take ya ov'r ta Genr'l

Cleburne's headquarters."

"Yes, Sir." Blake saluted and turned to the lieutenant.

"Come with me, Private." The two walked back to Blake's bedding area.

"Pack yer gear, Bradford." To those nearby Warren instructed, "Some'n take care a the drum. Private James is ridin courier agin."

Blake hefted his pack to his back, slung on his canteen and cartridge box, hung his rifle by its rawhide tie, and left with the lieutenant.

It was a long walk to the horse lines where the officer secured a healthy looking roan colored young stallion and ordered him saddled and prepared to go. Blake shifted his blanket roll to be tied to the back of the saddle. They left for the general's bivouac.

As the two approached the general's camp site on foot with the boy leading the horse, General Cleburne took notice and left his officers to meet them.

"Lieutenant," he began, "who have we here?"

"This is Private Bradford James, Sir. The captain has assigned him courier duty. He's ar drummer, but he's a good rider, too."

"I see you've been in combat," General Cleburne remarked noticing the bullet holes in the boy's uniform.

"Yes, Sir. I was ridin courier fer Colonel Butler at Richmond."

"He was killed ya know."

"Yes, Sir, I was with him"

"Lieutenant," Cleburne began, "Take Private James to General Hardee. He can use a battle experienced courier." To one of his orderlies he continued, "Captain, get this boy some saddle bags to he can get his pack off his back."

"Yes, Sir, General."

"Lieutenant, go with the captain and get the boy situated." To the orderly he continued, "and Captain, get a horse each for you and the lieutenant and take him to General Hardee with my compliments."

Captain George Nabors, a clean-shaven officer in his mid 20's, proved to be a capable, detail conscious officer. Checking the tack on the horse lines, he found a saddle with saddlebags, removed the saddle bags and helped the boy repack his gear while he selected two horses and instructed the lieutenant to supervise their preparation.

By late afternoon, Blake found himself in Major General William Hardee's command staff assigned to a staff officer in charge of the growing number of couriers arriving from the various divisions. That evening, sometime after dark, a cavalry general and his staff arrived to confer with General Hardee.

Blake was busy grooming his horse when General Joseph Wheeler and his staff rode by. He turned around, stood erect, and saluted the party. A staff officer returned the salute. The boy returned his attention to his horse.

"I ain't knowin yer name, but Roan 'll do if it's okay with ya." Blake had secured a comb from one of the stable help and caringly brushed the stallion's neck. "We're gonna ride together like Prince an me did back home," he whispered into Roan's ear. "We gotta be kerful. I don't want us gittin hurt 'r nothin."

Roan nuzzled the boy with his nose and earned a gentle scratching under his chin.

"Wished I had som'thin fer ya, but this land's so parched I ain't had nothing but hard tack an coffee. An I ain't sher thet coffee's made from water 'r mud. Tastes som'thin fierce." He stroked the strong neck and leaned his cheek against the firm head and felt the warmth. The two stood there a while longer. Blake patted the shoulder as he parted with, "See ya a bit later, Roan. Ya take care."

He left to return to his blanket near the fire around which other courier riders were gathered. The saddlebags with his gear were at the foot of his blanket and his rifle was tucked under the edge. Dropping his jacket and forage cap on the blanket near the head end, he settled in the quiet of his own thoughts sitting with his knees pulled up to his chin and his arms clasped around his ankles. In the quiet of that moment he felt so alone. He knew no one who was near by and really didn't care to. He wished he were with his company and friends he knew and would be there with his drum tomorrow to guide them through whatever events would unfold.

Footsteps approached.

"Private," an authoritative voice spoke up. "General Wheeler needs an experienced courier an General Hardee's staff officer says yer it."

Blake looked up into the face of a sharp, no nonsense captain who looked to be without emotion.

"Git yer gear, yer horse, an let's go." The officer stood, impatient to move on.

Quickly, the boy gathered his gear, carried it to his horse, saddled the horse, tied on his gear, and mounted to go.

"Follow me." The officer walked briskly and the boy followed on horseback. Arriving where the generals were deep in conversation, he said curtly, "Wait here." The officer left.

Blake dismounted and stood by his horse. He observed the two generals, seated on camp chairs near the fire, deep in conversation, their faces illuminated by the firelight. General Wheeler had a full dark beard, it even appeared somewhat curly along his jaw line, and a high forehead hairline. General Hardee's beard was mostly on his chin with a mustache. They were both hunched forward with their elbows on their knees as they spoke quietly to one another.

"Your plan to commence your attack early is critical," Wheeler pointed out. "Only Buell's advance corps under General Gilbert is on the Springfield Road nearest Perryville. Any delay and we'll have McCook and Crittenden's corps to deal with as well."

"My divisions are camped around us here," Hardee shared. "We are ready and will start first light."

"Crittenden is advancing along the Lebanon Pike. We'll meet him and prevent him from going around our left flank." Wheeler stood. "You found me an experienced courier?"

"He's just to the side there, Joe."

"But he's only a boy!" The general looked aghast.

"He's experienced, been in combat, a good horseman, and light for a good horse to make speed. And that stallion he has there looks like good thoroughbred stock."

"All good points, Bill. Be careful tomorrow, and don't forget, start early."

The two shook hands and parted. General Wheeler's staff quickly moved out to get to their horses and prepare to depart.

"Mount up, Private," the general ordered.

Blake was on his horse and following the general's staff immediately.

* * *

Blake was not the only courier. He was the youngest. He noticed others who weren't much older and most were small and wiry as he was. There would be no rest. The general and his staff were in the saddle and on the move the rest of the night, gathering information on the enemy corps approaching along the Lebanon Pike to the south of Perryville.

Hardee's army was to the north. General Polk's divisions were northwest of him. As the wee hours before dawn neared, Wheeler took his cavalry along the Lebanon Pike, westward toward the approaching Union corps under General Crittenden. Dawn came in all its heat and brilliance. The morning advanced as the cavalry patrolled in search of the enemy and the temperature raced into the 90s. To the north, there was silence. Around mid morning the battle opened in front for the cavalry.

A rider approached the general. "There ar enemy outposts jest a hundred yards up the pike," the trooper reported.

"Captain," Wheeler ordered, "take yer skirmish line forward and test their strength."

The company advanced, carbine rifles in hand. The crackle of gunfire opened and return fire could be heard from the enemy. The skirmishing grew intense as more troops were committed to the fight. The general pushed his command forward, slowly advancing on the enemy. The Federal troops held.

A new sound advanced from the front. Drums announced approaching infantry and artillery. Wheeler's bugler sounded recall and the skirmish line withdrew to reform and prepare for a larger attack. Enemy infantry opened fire as cannon were unlimbered and placed in line to support the infantry. Bullets whistled through the air like a swarm of bees, and several fell. Blake felt that familiar tugging of his uniform as some passed through his clothing. Roan remained calm and completely in the boy's control, as he guided his horse to stay with the general in the event there were orders to carry out. Several nearby were struck and a horse screamed in pain as a bullet tore through its hindquarter. The cavalrymen were firing back as the skirmishers returned and the brigade prepared to charge the enemy. A nearby trooper was struck in the neck and his lifeblood sprewed out onto Blake's uniform and the side of his face as the dying cavalryman fell from his horse.

The sound of bugles announced the arrival of enemy cavalry.

"Companies, form your lines," the general ordered. He drew his saber and held it high momentarily, then brought it forward. "Charge!" he commanded. The bugle sounded the charge and the brigade jumped into full gallop, headed toward the approaching cavalry.

Couriers followed along the back of the charge as the two cavalry brigades clashed in mortal combat with the clang of sabers and the explosion of carbines and some musketry from the line of infantry. There were the wild yelling of the charging armies mixed with the screams of pain from the wounded and dying and the shout of orders from the officers. As the battle continued, Blake was tempted to unsling his rifle from his shoulder and fire on the enemy. But even as he started to reach for his gun, he thought better of it and hung back with others from the staff.

There was a scream of pain nearby. "I'm hit!" an older boy slumped forward in his saddle and fell to the ground.

Blake quickly dismounted and led Roan to the boy's side. The boy lay conscious on the ground, shaking in shock and pain.

"Where?" the younger boy asked.

Unable to talk, he pointed to the side of his chest. Blake opened his coat to find a splotch of red flowing from a hole in the side of the uniform. A staff sergeant rushed to their side and quickly examined the wound while Blake held the boy in his lap.

"It went clean through," the sergeant announced as he pulled up the boy's shirt to see what could be done. "Cracked rib, but it may have missed his lung. Let's git him off the road and we'll hold him with the wounded until we kin send fer ambulance wagons. Private, ya best git back to the gen'ral."

Blake did as commanded, mounted his horse, and headed forward toward the general. The skirmish had moved down the road as the Union cavalry began to disperse and Wheeler's troops broke through the infantry and artillery. Shots rang out as the last of Wheeler's cavalry passed by. Several were hit. Few fell.

Blake felt the bullet slam into his shoulder and spin him out of his saddle. As he fell to the ground, he saw a union soldier run into the road, grab the loose reins of Roan's bridle and pull him off to the side of the road. Another young soldier ran from the ranks and scooped up the boy, rushing him into the Union ranks as the company quickly retired from the scene of combat.

The Union forces were driven from their guns and 140 prisoners were taken along with the remaining artillery pieces.

Recall was sounded and the brigade returned to reorganize for their next contact.

Blake found himself in the hands of the enemy.

* * *

"Sorry for grabbing you like that," the youth said as he lay Blake on the ground off the road. "I was afraid someone would run you down. You being the enemy, our people might trample you to death or run you over with an artillery piece." The young Union soldier tried to make Blake comfortable on the ground. "John has your horse. You look pretty bad, lots of blood. You hurt bad? Can you ride?"

"I don't know," Blake answered. "Hurts som'thin fierce."

"Matthew, we got to move," John stated. "The regiments moving on down the road." He tried to help Blake to his horse.

"Oww!" the boy cried.

An older sergeant approached the three.

"What the Hell you doing with this Reb trash?" he exclaimed. "Just leave him be and take his horse. I want his rifle." He reached to untangle the rifle from Blake's back.

"Ya keep off me!" Blake screamed, pushing away as the man grabbed the barrel of the gun.

"What's going on here?" a lieutenant asked as he came to investigate the commotion.

"Sergeant Carson is trying to steal this kid's rifle," John explained. "He was just shot and we're trying to help him."

"Sergeant, get back to your company," the lieutenant ordered. "I'll take care of things here."

"Thank ya, Lieutenant. My father gave me thet rifle fer ma tenth birthday." He spoke in tense pain. "It hurts, Sir!"

"Let me see, Son." Gently the officer slipped the jacket from the left shoulder leaving it hang from the good arm and examined the wound. "Lots of blood. It looks like the bullet passed through real close to the bone. It may be broke or cracked. We'll tie your arm down until a surgeon can take a look. Right now we have orders to move on south toward Mitchellsburg. I never thought to ask. What's your name, Boy?"

"Bradford James, Sir."

"These here are Privates Matthew Mills and John Timmons," he introduced. "I'm Lieutenant Thomas Kidner. I'll leave these boys to take care of you. But hurry. We have to move."

"There's a cloth in ma hav'sack I'd used fer food once."

John rummaged through the haversack and found the cloth. He folded it and tied it into a sling, then carefully eased Blake's arm into it.

"Can you ride?" Matthew asked. "If we can get you on your horse, I'll lead it," he offered.

Together, Matthew and John helped Blake onto Roan and they started off at an easy walk to catch up to their company.

* * *

Skirmishing continued along the road as the Confederate cavalry opened with its artillery and occasional charges against the Union division. Blake found himself in a company of the 31st Indiana. Their brigade's artillery periodically formed up and returned fire on the Confederates. Drums passed the orders throughout the division. A line of artillery was established and began firing against the enemy cavalry, sending shells overhead of the infantry troops gathering across the road.

"Mills," the lieutenant shouted above the roar and concussion of the guns, "You and Timmons take your friend toward the back. We're forming up to advance on the enemy."

Quickly the troops formed in line of battle. After firing one round and reloading, they began to advance against the Confederates. The cavalry withdrew a short distance then turned and fired. Some fell as muskets roared and fired again on the enemy. The advance continued.

"John, stay with Bradford," Matthew instructed as he rushed forward to assist one of the wounded.

The youth rushed forward to a soldier who was struggling to get to his feet. He found the man with a bullet wound to the side of his head. His scalp bled profusely.

"Here, let me help," the youth offered. "Take your coat off. I need your shirt sleeve."

The wounded soldier did as he was asked and slipped off his coat, relieved to get some fresh air. Matthew grabbed the top of his shirt sleeve and ripped it off.

"Why?" the man asked.

"I need it to bandage your head."

Slipping the fabric off the man's arm, Matthew wrapped the head wound and tied it tight. The soldier's hat lay on the ground. The boy gathered up the coat and hat and helped the soldier to his feet, then assisted him to walk back to the Federal line. Passing John, he handed him the coat and hat as he continued on with the wounded soldier.

"Here," he whispered. "Get these on Bradford." He moved on to take the injured man to the far side of the road where the wounded were being attended.

In the confusion of battle, John, a young man in his early twenties had taken the wounded boy and his horse behind the artillery line out of sight of the battery. "Bradford, give me our coat and hat and put these on." John laid the clothing across the back of Roan's neck in front of the saddle.

"Why fer?" the confused boy asked.

"Keep you from being taken off with the prisoners."

"Thanks."

The change was made as Matthew returned.

"What do we do with these?" John asked.

"He might need them later." Matthew untied the blanket roll from the back of the saddle. "Roll them in here then put them back."

John did as suggested.

The artillery had stopped to avoid striking their infantry. The enemy cavalry had fallen back and the division returned. The march toward Mitchellsburg continued.

As the company returned and the three fell back in line, Lieutenant Kidner joined them.

"What have we here, why the uniform change?"

Matthew responded, "We haven't been able to change our clothes since we left our knapsacks at Bowling Green last month and Bradford's jacket was all bloody. Besides," he lowered his voice, "he doesn't have to be sent off with the prisoners, does he?"

"You be careful, Matthew." The officer spoke quietly as well. "I know what this war has done to you and will do what I can to help. You need to watch out for Sergeant Carson."

"Yes, Sir."

"Now fall in with the company. As soon as you can, get him to a surgeon."

The man left to return to the order of march. The three privates took their place in their company and the division's move south.

* * *

The division settled in on the fields around Mitchellsburg, where they bivouacked and set their fires. Blake had been to see the surgeon who probed the wound and retrieved a small chip of bone. It was not broken, but would need time to mend. The boy had dropped his bedroll beside Matthew's but did not open it. It was too hot to climb in. He would use it as a pillow. Dinner had consisted of some roasted corn from the nearby fields and bacon. The coffee pot being the only cooking utensil carried, coffee was brewed. The soldiers had their cups and cooked their bacon using their ramrods to hang it over the fire. The three sat around the fire like the thousands around them, wrapped in quiet conversation.

"What did ya mean 'bout not havin yer knapsacks?" Blake asked.

"They were left at Bowling Green when we started after General Bragg's army," John explained.

"We haven't had any tents yet since last August when we left McMinnville in Tennessee," Matthew added. "You look around and you'll see men without blankets and some barefoot without shoes. In this heat, blankets have just been extra weight. But sooner or later this drought will break and the rain'll come and the cold, too."

"When we fust come up through Tennessee an lower Kentucy, we was short a ever'thin, too," Blake shared. "I come up with a supply train, but thet ran out fast. We really did good when we got the supply trains at Richmond and Lexington."

"Are you a drummer?" Matthew inquired.

"Yeh, but it were left in a supply wagon and I did courier duty."

"Christopher Jamison's our drummer," John volunteered. "We also have a fifer and a bugler. Their fire is up closer to the captain."

"We have to figure out how to get you into the company until we can get close enough for you to get back to your army." Matthew thought a minute. "I'll get an idea sometime."

"Why don't I jest enlist?" Blake suggested. "People from Kentucky ar jinin both armies."

"What about your uniform and your talking?" John asked.

"Ya said yerself, ya left yer packs behind. An when takin from a battlefield, ya git what ya kin. Talk? I jest come from a diff'rnt place."

"Come on," Matthew urged. "Let's go see the captain."

The three wandered along the line of campfires with their soldiers in conversation. As they approached the captain's fire, they were relieved to see the sergeant was no where around.

"Captain Ristine, Sir?" Matthew asked.

The captain turned from a conversation with cup in hand. "What is it, Private."

"This boy came up the road to us and wants to enlist." Matthew wasn't sure how this might go.

"Who are you, Boy? What happened to you? And what is that uniform?" The man sipped from his cup as he carefully studied the boy in front of him.

"I'm Bradford James, Sir. Bin follern the army some time now an pickin up uniform pieces from the fightin, whatever come close ta fittin. Got shot by some as didn't like ma uniform, I guess. But it'll be all right."

"You don't talk like us."

"We's from differ'nt places, Sir."

"Your not old enough."

"Am fer a drummer."

"Can you play?" The captain was getting impatient with the easy flow of answers and a nagging uncertainty about the whole effort.

"Yes, Sir."

"Private Jamison!" he called. "Bring your drum and come here."

The drummer arrived quickly. "Yes, Sir?"

"I want to hear this boy play."

The fourteen-year-old handed Blake his strap and drum, then drumsticks. Blake adjusted the drum to a comfortable position, then struck a cadence. A moment later he went into the long roll and, wincing with pain, finished with taps.

The captain was dumbfounded.

"You're good!" the drummer exclaimed.

"Lieutenant," the captain turned to Kidner, who had observed all without a word. "Add Private Bradford James to the muster roll. You can work with Private Jamison as needed. Move your bedding with the musicians."

"Kin Mills an Timmons come, too? They he'ped git ma arm fixed."

"Okay. See to it Lieutenant."

The lieutenant walked with them as they went to retrieve their bedding. "You three are cleaver. What will the sergeant do when he finds out?"

"Jest tell him as I changed sides."

* * *

Roan had been left tied to a tree in the woodlot beside the fields. Blake retrieved him and brought him to the camp and ground tied him at the head of his bedding, simply by dropping the reins. The captain arrived immediately to ask about the horse.

"Where did this horse come from, Private?" His voice was a mix of anger and curiosity.

"Found him comin up the road. I was ridin him when I was shot." Blake stood holding the bridle and stroking Roan's muzzle. "Kin I keep him?"

"He'd be good for courier," the drummer volunteered. "Look, he has an army saddle so he's probably trained."

"Good idea, Private. Private James, he's your responsibility."

"Yes, Sir. I'll do real good by him."

The captain returned to his fire.

A distant bugle sounded. The company bugler picked up the call and repeated it. Lowering his horn he turned to meet the new musician.

"I'm Private Beverly McDonald. Just call me Bev." He offered his hand.

"Private McDonald," the captain called. "Take that horse and ride over to see what the general wants."

Blake took a fast handshake as Beverly hung the bugle over his shoulder and walked to the horse. With his good hand, Blake patted Roan on the neck then handed the reins to the bugler and watched him leave. "His name's Roan," he whispered as the two departed.

The sun had dipped beyond the treetops as the boy knelt to add some wood to the fire. Matthew introduced Blake to the fifer, Timothy Sanderson and the five settled by the fire to await the bugler's return. It wasn't long. A horse made a difference and the captain appeared to be appreciative.

Captain Ristine announced to his officers, "We are to move back toward Perryville in the morning and prepare to renew the attack on Bragg's army. Pass the word for the men to get some sleep and we'll start at first light."

The sun settled below the horizon and daylight dimmed. As day passed into night, the landscape took on a new brilliance as a full moon rose into the night sky. Drummers struck taps throughout the camp, still, many remained by their fires to gaze about the landscape of men and fires, wrapped in whispered conversations mixed with the songs of crickets and tree toads.

* * *

The following morning it was discovered that Bragg's army had left Perryville and was headed south. Brigadeer General William Smith was sent with his division toward Stanford, but any attempt to catch the enemy was called off and General Buell began to work the rest of his army toward Nashville, Tennessee. Smith's division continued to the southeast. As the month advanced the weather finally broke and the rains began in the later half, and the temperatures finally dropped. Through Wild Cat on the 17th, they were at London by the 22nd. The Salt Works at Goose Creek were destroyed on the 23rd and 24th as the division left London and started back toward Mount Vernon.

At 6AM on Saturday, October 25th, Jamison struck Reveille. Again, Blake awoke to wet blankets, but this time they were white. It was the first snow of the season.

"Matthew," he called, "it's snowin!" Quickly the boy shook his blanket of its snow, stuffed his grey uniform inside, and rolled them into the gum blanket to tie onto his pack which he had removed from the saddlebags along with his personal gear, and repacked to carry. Nearly two weeks had passed since Perryville and his shoulder had healed enough to remove the sling and carry his equipment.

"This stuff's coming down fast," John observed. "It's bad enough I have to tie my shoes together to keep them from falling off, some of these guys don't have anything and have to walk barefoot in it."

"Private Jamison," the captain ordered, "sound assembly. We have to get on the road so we can get past Mount Vernon today."

The division was assembled and began its trek to Mount Vernon. By the time they were on the road, the men were walking through six inches of snow. It wasn't six inches for long. As the thousands passed it was trampled into a muddy roadway. At Mount Vernon the soldiers halted for an hour for dinner, then took the southwest road to Somerset. Five miles beyond they made camp for the night in a meadow.

Matthew gazed about the fields. "This is great. They've begun the harvest and we have acres of straw and hay."

The men and boys gathered all the straw and hay they could use and prepared their bedding for the night.

"This is heavenly!" Beverly exclaimed. "I wish we could stay here a week!"

The snow had stopped and the army slept a peaceful and comfortable night.

In the days ahead the army passed Sumerset and moved on to Columbia, arriving there on the 31st. Staying there a day, they were able to draw some shoes and shirts for the men. The following day their wagons finally caught up to them. They were able to pitch their tents again, retrieve their knapsacks, and change their clothes for the first time in six weeks. Over the next few days, traveling from Columbia to Bowling Green, the divisions of the army came together. On Saturday, November 8th, the army finally arrived at Nashville, Tennessee, and settled in for the winter.

Blake, Matthew, John, and the musicians had become fast friends.

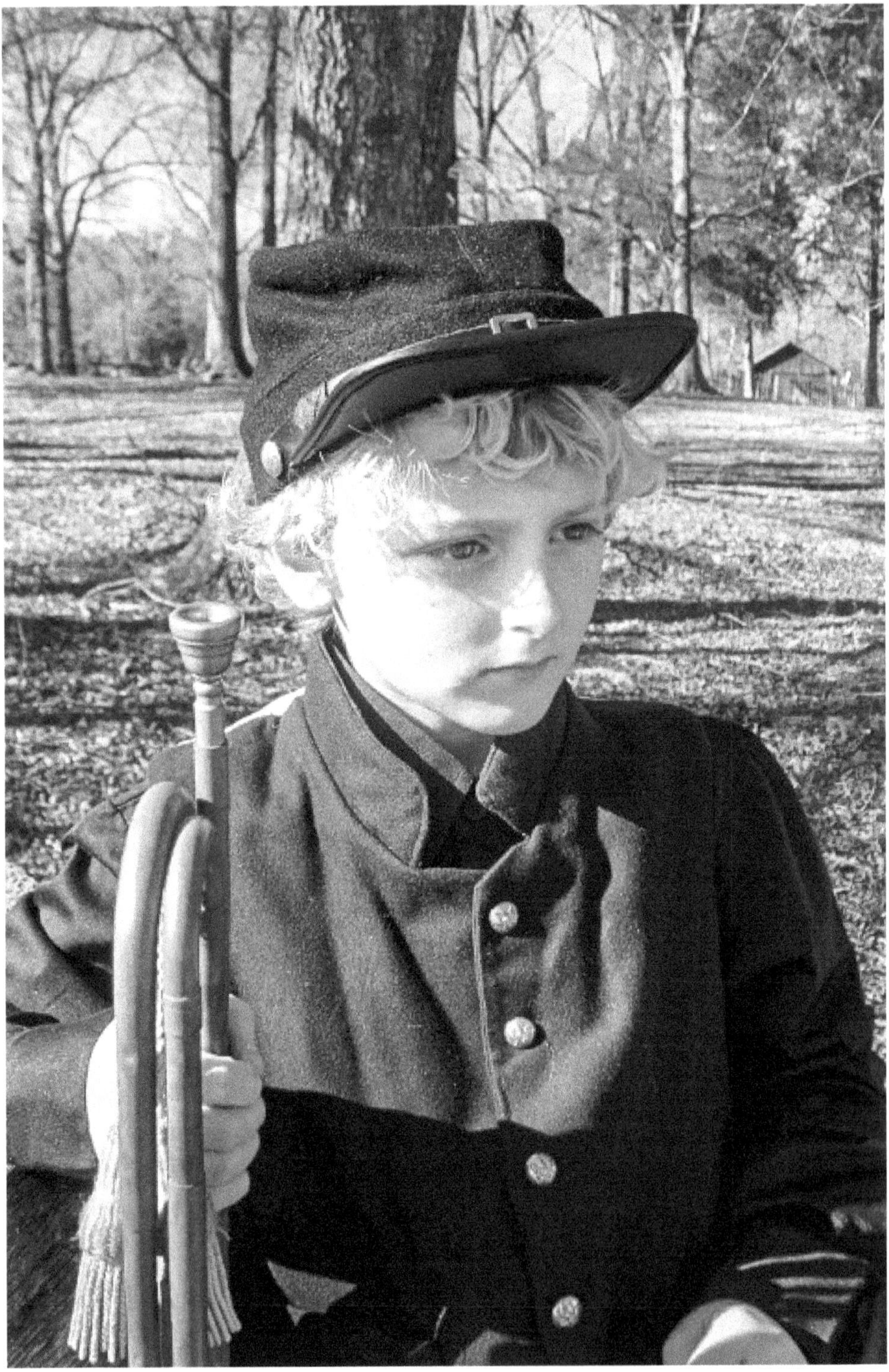

Chapter Five
A Battle at Stones River

"Bradford," John called as he burst into the tent. "Matthew and Christopher are wanting to go hunting in the fields west of here. We just want to get out of camp for something different. Will you come with us?"

"Sher. We bin here nigh ta two weeks an we mostly drill an do guard duty or some work detail." Blake took up his cartridge box, cap box, rifle , and haversack. "I think I'm ready."

The two walked out to join their friends and work their way out of the camp.

It was their second Saturday encamped around Nashville. The camp was near the edge of the city, a vast sprawl of 17,000 souls located alongside the Cumberland River, a transportation center for river and railroad traffic. But river traffic was hindered by low water levels and railroad traffic was hindered by Confederate raids to destroy track and bridges. Rations were meager and supplementing the diet was welcome when possible.

Blake now had a complete Union uniform and had packed his into the saddlebags he had been given. His horse was gone. Roan had been taken to the stock pens where all the division's horses were kept. The saddlebags were with his gear in the tent. Camp tents were better than those used in the field, they were high enough to stand up in. The troops had also been issued additional blankets since going into camp. At least they could sleep warmer.

John was the old man in the group at twenty-two. Matthew was next at eighteen. Christopher was fourteen, and Blake, at eleven, was the youngest. They varied in height, but had one thing in common. They were all skin and bones for lack of food.

A light snow drifted in the air. The boys shivered in the cold, but were used to it. Snow crunched underfoot as the four left the camp behind and approached the fields.

"Da ya think ther'll be eny game?" Blake asked. "It sher is grey an dark lookin."

"I hope so," Matthew stated.

"Let's go slow and check for tracks," John suggested.

The hunters moved slowly along the edge of the fields, watching closely for any sign of tracks. Matthew and Blake followed one side of the road and John with Christopher followed the other.

Suddenly Christopher pointed and whispered. "I think I see something near the edge of that bush."

The four studied a dark shadow. After a while, it moved, then stopped again.

"I think it's a fox," John whispered. "Probably hunting like we are."

"I kin eat fox," Blake suggested.

"Hardly enough for us all," Christopher observed.

"Doesn't matter unless we shoot it," John added.

Matthew raised his gun, taking careful aim, and squeezed the trigger. The shot echoed across the fields off the trees in the woods. The animal dashed for safety.

"Guess we don't have to worry about it," Matthew reflected. "I missed."

The four turned back to the road and continued on. The bleak landscape offered no other sign of life. An hour passed and cold crept in. They approached a farm lane. There was no sign of life, no tracks, and glancing at the distance farmhouse, no chimney smoke. Standing there, the boys gazed at the house and wondered.

"Do you think there's anyone there?" Christopher wondered out loud.

"We could look," Matthew suggested.

Blake started up the lane. The others followed. Closer to the buildings they observed drifted over tracks between the house and the barn. Chickens chattered inside the barn and a cow lowed softly. There was the clatter of a bucket and the pawing of a hoof.

The four entered the barn and were surprised to find an older man milking a cow. He was startled as he suddenly realized someone had entered and quickly stood up and turned. Without warning, he put the bucket down and grabbed a nearby hay fork.

"Ya ain't got no business here. There's nothin more ta take. I need it fer ma family."

"We didn't know anyone was here," John explained. "We just came in to look. There's no chimney smoke or sign of life."

"Ar fire went out an we ain't nothin ta start it agin." He stood, frightened, still holding the fork.

"Maybe we can help," Matthew offered.

"How." He stood the fork against the cow's stall.

John looked around the barn and had an idea. "You have straw and wood scrap and firewood?"

"Yes."

"I think I have fire." All looked at the youth as though he were crazy.

"Whar?" Blake asked.

"My gun." All looked and wondered. "If we set the stove with lots of wood scrap and straw and I only put powder in my gun, when I fire it there should be a flame come out."

"Yea," the others chorused.

John stepped outside the barn, aimed toward the fields, and fired his gun. The shot echoed off the buildings and a woman and her children came running from the house to see what was wrong.

She had a shotgun in hand.

"It's all right, Hannah. They're here ta he'p."

The man explained what was happening and the children rushed to gather straw and wood scraps from the barn floor. Then all headed toward the house and crowded into the kitchen. The man piled straw and wood scraps into the kitchen stove while John reloaded his rifle with two cartridges of powder and no bullets. He placed the cap on the nipple and pulled back the hammer. Placing the muzzle in the stove against the straw, he pulled the trigger. The blast concussion caught everyone by surprise as it pressed against their ears and the flame out the barrel rushed into the straw and set it ablaze. Quickly more straw was added and the flame began to catch on the scraps. The family had fire.

"Now you can use some long wood strips to light your lamps," Christopher suggested.

"We're truly grateful," the man said. "How kin we he'p ya?"

"We're hungry an was huntin, but couldn't git anythin," Blake explained.

"Would some potatoes an carrots an a chicken he'p?" the woman asked.

"We'd sure like that," Matthew replied.

"Ya yunguns take this boy an fill his hav'sack from the root cellar an yer pa an me 'll kill an clean a chicken."

* * *

"You said your teacher taught you how to play the bugle?" Beverly asked.

"He showed me some military calls an some tunes." The boy warmed his hands by the fire.

Sunday was cold, but the snow had stopped. The musicians had gathered to play together and Blake and his friends sat with them around the fire.

"Want to play?" the bugler offered.

Blake took the bugle, put it to his lips, and started a lively tune. Christopher and Timothy joined in and the air filled with their music. When the piece had ended, Timothy offered his fife.

"I ain't good with thet," Blake declined.

The others chuckled at the admission.

"Our turn," Beverly said, and the three musicians set out to play a number of their favorite tunes.

Sergeant Carson approached the fire. "Got a job for you all," he started. "Time to work off that fine meal you had last night. Get axes and a saw from the supply tent and get a day's supply of firewood for each of the fires in the staff area." There was a look of smug satisfaction as he turned back to his fire.

The musicians put their instruments in their tent and joined the other three at the supply tent where they picked out their tools and headed toward a nearby park to cut down a tree. A local boy saw the boys walking toward the park with their cutting tools and ran to get his friends. By the time the six arrived, a gang of local youths had gathered. One had his pa's army revolver.

"Ya all ain't cuttin eny more a ar trees," he shouted, pointing the gun at the wood cutting detail.

"You put that away before someone gets hurt," John ordered.

"I ain't takin orders from ya Yank trash." He pulled back the hammer. "Git em boys."

A dozen local boys charged the young soldiers.

"Stand back!" John ordered as he turned the saw blade toward he attackers. Timothy and Blake each had an ax and turned their blades toward the oncoming boys. They stopped. The gun went off, its roar echoing through the trees and bouncing off nearby buildings.

One of the local boys flew forward, landing face down in the snow. He made no sound. He made no movement. There was stunned silence. The youth stood there in shock as smoke curled from the barrel of the gun.

"Jimmy!" another boy screamed as he dropped in the snow beside his friend.

John dropped the saw and walked toward the fallen boy.

"Don't ya tuch him!" The hammer clicked back on the revolver.

The other boys turned around. One fifteen-year-old shouted, "Ya put thet gun down, Calvin! Yer finished!"

As some of the older boys advanced on Calvin and he turned and ran, John knelt to see how bad the boy on the ground was hurt. Matthew joined him.

Blood soaked the back of Jimmy's coat below his right shoulder. The friend sat back on his heals, crying as John and Matthew checked the wound. Jimmy didn't move.

"Does anyone know if there's a doctor near here?" John looked up into the faces of the remaining boys.

Matthew noticed the snow near Jimmy's nose. "He's alive," he announced. "The snow is melted near his nose. He's breathing."

"My pa's a doctor," one of the younger boys answered.

"Take us to him?" John asked, to Matthew he instructed, "Help me get him up real careful like." As they lifted Jimmy off the ground and rolled him over into John's arms, John instructed, "You all start on the wood cutting. The sergeant wouldn't understand. We'll be back as soon as we get Jimmy some help."

The remaining gang of boys followed as the doctor's son led John and Matthew to his house.

* * *

The sergeant stood watching as the last of the firewood was stacked by his fire site. He had noticed the blood on John's jacket, "You boys have an accident?" he smirked.

"It's taken care of," John responded. They turned and left toward their own fire.

It had taken most of the day to cut and collect the firewood. There was no time to talk about the incident or share the results of the older boys' trip to the doctor's. They worked together silently to build up their fire and prepare a pot of coffee. Christopher put the coffee beans in the old sock and held it on a nearby stump as Timothy took a rock and crushed them. Beverly filled the pot from a nearby bucket of water and hung it from the cross rack over the fire. The sock was dropped in and the lid placed on the pot.

They settled on assorted empty food crates by the fire.

"How bad is Jimmy?" Beverly asked.

"The bullet was still in there," Matthew explained. "It hit his shoulder bone and cracked it."

"The doctor dug it out and put a bandage on and the arm in a sling," John continued. "He said there was nothing else he could do."

"What 'bout Calvin?" Blake asked.

"We don't know," Matthew said.

"These people hate us so much," Timothy acknowledged.

"I hate this war," Matthew volunteered. "I can't stand the killing and hurting."

The coffee pot started to boil and steam. John took a cloth and lifted the pot from its hanger. The others offered their cups and he filled them, then his own, and rehung the pot. Each sipped from his cup in silence.

Lieutenant Kidner approached the group.

"You boys did a nice job collecting firewood," he offered. "Tomorrow while the rest of the company is at drill, I need you to go with me to the wharfs to load some wagons with provisions from the riverboats. The river's come up enough for them to start to get through." He noticed the blood on John's jacket. "Did one of you get hurt?" he asked.

"We took care of it," John replied.

No more was said.

"Christopher," the lieutenant continued. "Time for meal call."

The drummer went to his tent, strapped on his drum, and struck the call.

* * *

On Monday, the musicians and friends went with the lieutenant to the wagon park and stock yards to get teams and three wagons for the supply run. Kidner was able to get Roan for himself to ride for the day. Blake was delighted to see his old friend again, and the horse remembered the boy.

The wharf was alive with excitement and activity. A dozen steamboats lay moored along the shore while hundreds of stevedores unloaded mountains of crates and barrels of hardtack, flour, sugar, molasses, and whiskey. The provisions were being picked up by wagons sent from encampments all around Nashville. From time to time trains would get through on the Nashville and Chattanooga Railroad bringing soldiers' rations, each a day's provisions for one soldier; blankets, shoes, and tents for distribution throughout the camps as well as supply trains serving the armies on the move beyond the city.

The days slipped by. Nashville had a theater. One Saturday the boys tried it out and saw a production of Shakespeare's Hamlet. There was a graveyard scene. In it Hamlet found the skull of Yorick. As he raised it up, a soldier in the back of the audience shouted, "Hey, Pard, what is it – Yank or Reb?" The audience roared with laughter. "What jest happ'ned?" Blake wondered. "They're laughing at what the soldier said." "Oh."

As November drifted into December, trouble continued in the countryside outside the city. Word came in that Confederate guerilla fighters had removed the passengers from five riverboats and burned the boats. In another instance, raiders wrecked a train then shot at the people on the train.

The army in Nashville stayed put and continued to drill. General Rosecrans, who had replaced General Buell when the army was on the march from Perryville to Nashville, continued to gather and train troops until he was satisfied the army was ready to go after the Confederate army. The Confederate army had retreated from Perryville by way of Knoxville and Chatanooga and had ended up at Murfreesboro, about forty miles southeast of Nashville.

* * *

During the first week of December, Christopher developed a cough. It got worse. As he sat by the fire Friday morning at breakfast, he couldn't stop shaking.

- 83 -

"Ya ain't gittin no better," Blake observed. "We gotta git ya ta the hospital."

"Not going," Christopher stated firmly. "Most people who go to the hospital end up dying. I have to get warm." He shivered uncontrollably.

"We have to get him more blankets," Matthew suggested.

"Ther's extra in the supply tent," Blake stated.

Matthew thought a minute. He knew the captain wouldn't let the boys have them. He reached over and touched his friend's forehead. "Your burning up!"

"But I'm freezing!"

"Sarah always said as ya have ta sweat the fev'r out from a person," Blake shared.

"Who's Sarah?" the drummer boy asked.

"She's ar house servant who knows the most doct'rin."

"That settles it," Matthew said. "We're getting those blankets."

"When the cap'n calls fer fust muster, I'll do Christopher's drummin an says as he's sick an yer with him. Ya sneak in the back a the supply tent an git the blankets."

"Okay."

"I gotta git his drum."

Blake walked to the musicians' tent and retrieved the drum with its strap and sticks. He also brought the drummer's blankets.

"Here, put these on him fer now."

The two opened the blankets and wrapped them around their friend's shoulders.

"Private, sound assembly," Lieutenant Kidner ordered.

Blake reported to the captain's tent and struck the call. As the long roll echoed through the camp, Sergeant Carson made sure all responded.

"Where's Privates Mills and Jamison," he asked peering at Blake.

"Jamison's sick an Mills is takin care a him," Blake responded.

Knowing Carson, Lieutenant Kidner went to check. He returned to report to the Captain. "Captain, Jamison is burning up with fever and Mills is tending to him by the fire."

"Very well," the captain instructed, "let them be reported as accounted for." He proceeded to inspect the line.

Matthew crept into the back of the supply tent and grabbed up a half dozen wool blankets, then carefully worked his way back to the musicians' tent. Depositing them inside, he returned to the fire before anyone realized he had left it. The troops were instructed to replenish their firewood supplies and dismissed.

"Can you guys get us firewood so Bradford can help me with Christopher?" Matthew asked.

"We'll take care of it," John replied. As they left, the two helped their friend into his tent and rearranged his bedding. Two blankets were spread on the ground. Christopher was placed on top fully clothed. The rest of the blankets were placed on top of him and tucked in under his body. The two waited to see if it would work.

"I'm cold settin here," Blake complained.

"Me, too,"

"Let's git ar blankets and wrap up agin him."

"You stay," Matthew said. "I'll get them."

The two wrapped up in their own blankets then lay down on either side of their patient as close as they could get. An hour passed. The others returned with the firewood. Wondering where their friends had gone, Beverly entered the tent in search.

"What are you doing?" he asked.

"Bradford said we should try to sweat the sickness out of him," Matthew explained.

"I've heard of that, too," the fifer stated. "But our drummer is going to have to do his duty. I'll take over then."

The hours passed; at some point Christopher stopped shaking and slept. John and Beverly kept the fire going and the coffee hot. Blake slipped out for meal call then afternoon muster. Beverly did colors, and dinner. Sergeant Carson showed up to see where everyone was.

He saw the pile of blankets. "You are going on report and are in so much trouble." He left. Shortly thereafter another came.

"What's going on here?" a voice approached the tent. Lieutenant Kidner stepped inside. "What's this about blankets being stolen?"

"We jest borrowed them ta he'p Private Jamison git well," Blake explained.

"How is that?" the officer asked.

"We're trying to sweat it out of him," Matthew explained.

"When you're finished, I expect to find them accounted for in the supply tent." He left.

Christopher slept through it all. Darkness fell. Blake was called to sound taps. All six of the friends piled close to each other for the night.

* * *

"Hey. What are you guys doing? It's so hot in here and I'm soaking wet with sweat." Christopher tried to push the weight off of him.

"How to you feel," Matthew asked.

"I'm hot!"

"Yer cough?" Blake asked.

"Don't have one."

Everyone backed off and helped to peel the blankets off the drummer.

"Yer soakin wet," Blake observed.

"Your clothes are wet clear through," John said as he ran his hands on the younger boy's body. "You put on a dry change of clothes before you get sick again."

"We'll lay these blankets out to dry, if they don't freeze first, then take them back to the lieutenant," Matthew stated.

Beverly stood up, keeping his blanket on cloak fashion. "It's cold. Let's get the fire up so we can cook breakfast." He and John left to tend the fire.

Christopher quickly stripped out of his wet clothes and pulled on dry johns and uniform. Just in time.

"Reveille!" the sergeant called.

* * *

Matthew, Blake, and Christopher started off with a saw and an ax.

"We're goin ta the park fer firewood," Blake announced.

"We'll be along shortly to help carry it back," Timothy called out.

The three left and headed up the street. The park lay a quarter mile from the camp. Once a heavily wooded and beautiful area, half of its trees were gone. In another four weeks it would be stripped bare and the soldiers would have to go much further for future wood gathering.

Suddenly, a wet mass splashed against Blake's face and another quickly followed on Matthew's shoulder. The boys stopped to see who threw them. The local gang was lined up on the far side of the street. One with his arm in a sling stood with them.

"We hate Yanks!" Jimmy shouted. "But some are toler'ble!"

His friends let loose a barrage of snowballs. The boys dropped their tools and scooped up handfuls of snow to strike back. At first the two groups just fired at each other back and forth across the street. The larger group then armed themselves and charged across the roadway with their own version of the Rebel Yell.

"Run!" Matthew cried.

They grabbed their tools and charged toward a fallen tree with an ample layer of snow on top. Hopping across the tree, they dropped behind and started arming themselves with snowballs and firing back. Jimmy held off to the side as his friends charged the tree. They were soon over the top and the melee fell to hand to hand snow rubbed into each other's face. It progressed to grabbing each other and rolling in the snow until all were thoroughly covered.

There was a brief pause as they stood up and brushed the snow off. Suddenly the local boys found themselves under attack from behind. John and the others had arrived and figured out what was happening, and decided to join the fun. When the gang turned to fire back, Blake and his friends decided to take advantage and open fire again. The local boys were caught in the middle. But there were more of them and they simply divided into two groups, each firing in the opposite direction. Once again they charged their opponents with their Rebel Yell. Again they clashed and rolled on the ground with the enemy. The battle ended and all stood to brush off the snow.

"Thet looked splendid!" Jimmy exclaimed.

"It were sher fun," one of his friends added. "You fellers ain't so bad."

"You're okay, too." Matthew continued, "I hate this war. I wish we could just be friends."

"Maybe some day," John spoke up. "For now we need to get our firewood. I really wish it weren't this park and that after the war, it will grow back."

"Kin I cum with ya?" Jimmy asked.

"Sher!" Matthew responded quickly. "How will you get home?"

"I kin find ma way in the mornin?" he asked hopefully. "T'wuld be neat ta camp out."

"What 'bout yer pa?" Blake asked.

"He's gon ta the war an Ma won't mind if she knows I'm safe." Jimmy turned to his friend. "Malicah, tell my ma as I'm with the soldier as saved ma life an 'll be home cum mornin."

"Sher." He turned and started off with the rest of the gang.

"Will you be okay while we cut our firewood?" John asked.

"Why don't you wear my coat while I'm working?" Timothy offered.

"Thanks," Jimmy replied. "I'll jest set a spell on this here tree. Ya all pretty much cleaned off the snow."

Jimmy settled onto the tree as his new friends proceeded to gather the firewood needed for the next day.

* * *

The fire crackled noisily as the seven sat around and sipped on their hot tins of coffee. It was particularly cold and each had brought out a blanket to wrap around him. The lieutenant had authorized the loan of two blankets for Jimmy. The small boy with his right arm in a sling, sat wrapped in the blankets, sipping from a warm tin of coffee, sitting contentedly beside Blake.

"Matthew," Blake asked, "what happened ta ya as the lieutenant said when we fust met?"

There was silence as all but Blake and Jimmy knew the answer and knew also that Matthew didn't want to talk about it.

"Tell you another time. It hurts too much." A sudden sadness crept into his voice and a quiet tear slipped free.

"Yer not like I 'spected. It's like taday an Jimmy here an the other boys in the snowball fight. Yer people jest like back home. Yer friends. I thought I hated Yanks. But wer all in this doin what wer told an some as wished we could be friends. Ya saved ma life when ya coulda let yer army kill me."

Surprise registered on Jimmy's face. "Yer a Reb?" he asked softly.

"Yea," Blake confirmed quietly.

"I shot a Reb," Matthew barely whispered. "It was my first battle and I thought I could kill Rebs. But I shot my first Reb, and as soon as I pulled the trigger, I got sick and fell to the ground. The lieutenant knows I will never kill again if I can help it. He knows, too, that I will save a life when I can, no matter the army. I think that's why he let me help you. None of us likes the killing. These guys are musicians and aren't expected to kill. But John and me are supposed to be soldiers." His voice faded.

"Why are you in this war?" Christopher asked.

This time Blake was caught off guard and didn't want to answer. He hesitated a long time. All sipped their coffee in silence, and waited.

Jimmy watched his young friend's face and saw an unexpected hurt.

"My father was kilt at Shiloh," he began, then stopped. The boy remained silent for several minutes. No one spoke. Then he simply stated, "I thought I wanted ta kill Yanks." That was all. He said no more.

The conversation was painful for all and they let it end.

Jimmy stared into the fire as he realized he had listened to a conversation revealing a truth about these young soldiers so very different than what he expected. Suddenly he knew what Blake had just observed, they really were so much alike. They really could be friends. It was the war that made them seem different. But they really weren't.

* * *

It was Tuesday of the third week of December when the bugle call was heard from the regimental bugler.

"Bradford," the captain ordered.

"Yes, Sir." The boy hurried to the captain's tent.

"Run over to regimental command and find out what our orders are."

"Yes, Sir. On ma way."

Blake ran through the camps of the regiment until he arrived at Colonel Osborn's headquarters. The colonel's staff officer instructed the messengers that there was to be a division review by General Rosecrans at two o'clock in the afternoon. Prepare your camps, and division muster will be at one o'clock. Blake rushed back to report the news to the captain.

"Private Jamison, sound assembly," the captain ordered.

The drum rolled, as others rolled throughout the camps, and the company assembled to receive instructions for the review. The camp was to be thoroughly cleaned and all tents and gear in perfect order. Each was to be in cleanest possible uniform, weapons clean, gear in good order, cartridge boxes full. Sergeant Carson would be around for any in need of cartridges and caps. Activity was intense as each soldier went about attending to the orders. Noon meal was called, to be taken cold from provisions in the haversack.

As the musicians gathered, they were in full uniform with all their gear for the first time since the march back from Perryville. Again Blake marveled at how sharp they looked, especially with their musician's swords worn on the left side of their belts. He had only seen them in use during that march and that was to cook their bacon over the fire as the men had used their ramrods. Since entering Nashville the swords had been stored with their other gear. They hadn't needed them until this day's review.

"Do ya eve use yer swords?" Blake asked.

"We're hardly ever close enough," Timothy replied. "But once I used it to help dig a fire pit when we were in camp on the way to Perryville."

"Back in May when we were in Corinth rounding up what Rebs we could find, I used mine to trip a Johnny who was running by trying to escape capture," Christopher added. "Just reached it between his feet while he ran past."

"Yeh, you should have seen the look on his face when Christopher put the point on his chest and told him he was his prisoner." Beverly laughed at the memory as the others chuckled, too.

"We'll pull them during the review," Timothy explained, "for present arms as the general goes by, and hold the tip near our shoulder." He demonstrated. "That's about all."

"Here," Christopher offered as he drew his sword and handed it to Blake. "Take a look. It's not heavy and only gets in the way sometimes when you try to sit down."

Blake took the weapon and turned it over in his hands, then stepped away and made a practice downward thrust. Glancing ahead he saw Jimmy approaching, took the blade in his hand, and offered the hilt back to Christopher who slipped it back into its sheath.

Jimmy had visited the camp on several occasions since the day of the snowball battle. He had become close friends with Blake and Matthew. On this day he arrived in time for noon meal and brought along some fresh-baked sweet cakes from home. He wore an oversized dark coat which covered his hands and helped to keep them warm, and carried a cloth sack for the cakes.

"Hi," he greeted wandering into camp. "What's all the excitement?"

John glanced up from the fire where he was pouring a cup of coffee. "We're getting ready for a division inspection by the general. Want some coffee." He presented a cup of warm dark liquid.

"Thanks," Jimmy accepted. "Here's some cakes fer ev'ryone." He handed the sack to John, then took a seat near the fire.

"Yer jest in time," Blake observed. "These'll be much better then ar hardtack." He accepted a cake from John as the youth opened the bag and handed them out.

"How's your arm coming?" Beverly asked between mouthfuls of cake.

"Johnny's pa says as it's doin good. But it'll be afta the new year b'fer I kin git rid a the sling."

At 12:30 the drums began to roll throughout the division.

"Sound assembly!" the sergeant ordered.

"Follow alongside us as we move out," Timothy instructed. "When we get to the division's fields, find a place along the edge and wait for us, then meet us back here."

"I'll do as ya says," the ten-year-old stated as he stood aside to watch the company assemble, and Beverly finished strapping on his drum and moved to the captain's tent.

The companies assembled and marched to their regimental formations. Musicians were gathered at the front of their regiments as the regimental musicians struck their cadence and music for the march and maneuvered to brigade formation. The air filled with the shouts of orders, the instructions from drums and bugles, the sound of thousands marching in unison, with the rhythmic music of regimental field music corps. There were masses of movement as regiments assembled, moved into brigade formation, then gathered in division formation. By one o'clock the division was gathered on the fields beside division headquarters. The gathering settled and the music stopped.

Jimmy had found a place on the field's edge, as close to the 31st Indiana as he could get. He watched in awe as the thousands stood in quiet formation awaiting the arrival of the general.

In the silence, General Rosecrans on his dappled grey, accompanied by his staff, rode on to the edge of the field and proceeded to ride the ranks and inspect his army. It was an impressive sight. The affair lasted the afternoon and the troops were dismissed just before 4 PM. It was close to five o'clock before the companies had returned to their camps. Weapons were stacked in lines in front of the tents as the drums sounded dinner call and meals were prepared on the various campfires.

"Would you like something to eat before you go," the fifer asked. "It's not much, but it's hot." He offered some bacon to go with the hard bread.

"Thanks," the boy accepted. He took the piece of sizzling meat from the outstretched pan and a piece of hard bread from a nearby plate.

Without warning, a shot rang out partway through the camp as a musket fell to the ground and went off. "Corporal Richards is hit!" the call went out. Quickly friends gathered to learn the extent of the man's injury. "The bullet is lodged in his arm," was the report.

"We need a doctor," the captain announced. "Where's the nearest hospital?"

Matthew reported, "I know where there's a doctor. His house is nearby."

"Go and get him," Ristine ordered.

"Bradford," Matthew asked. "You and Jimmy come with me."

Quickly, Jimmy stuffed the meat in his mouth as the three left at a slow run, the youth leading the way.

"Who?" Blake asked.

"Johnny's pa," Jimmy stated after swallowing the bacon. He shoved the bread into his pocket. "He's the doctor who took car a me when Matthew took me thet day."

Just past the park, Matthew turned down a street to the right.

"I'll git home from here," Jimmy announced. "Hope yer friend'll be okay."

"Thanks," Matthew replied. "See you tomorrow."

As the small boy disappeared into the dark, the remaining two approached a large house a block down on the left and knocked on the door. The young boy from the gang opened the door.

"Is your pa home," the youth asked.

"What is it, Johnny?" the man called from within.

"It's the boy who he'ped bring Jimmy the other week."

The man came to the door. "What is it?" he asked.

"A friend's been shot. Can you help?" Matthew replied.

"I'll git ma bag." Turning back to grab his medical bag, he returned and they left the house. "How fer?"

"The army camp about a quarter mile."

The three hurried to the camp. They were met by the captain.

"What happened?"

"The gun fell and went off," the captain explained. "The bullet lodged in his arm."

The table under the tarp in front of the captain's tent became the operating area as Richards sat on a camp stool with his arm resting on the table. Darkness had set in and lamps were lit. The doctor opened his bag and took out his probe. The bullet was soon found and removed and the wound was bandaged.

"Watch fer infection. If there is any, git him ta one a the hospitals quick." Wiping the probe with a cloth in his bag, he put it away and closed the bag. "I'll find ma way home."

He turned and left, quickly fading into the night.

* * *

First muster had been dismissed when Matthew turned to Blake. "Bradford, I have an idea." He pulled the boy aside. "Let's go see that doctor and find out where we can get some medical stuff to be able to help the wounded on the battlefield."

"Good idea."

The two told the lieutenant they needed to see the doctor for some information, then left the camp toward the park and the doctor's house. It was daylight so they could see the sign when they arrived. Johnny answered the door again and Blake asked, "Kin we see Doctor Darlington?"

The man heard his name and the familiar voices and came to the door. "What da ya need?" he asked.

"Do you know where we can get bandages and stuff to help wounded soldiers on the battlefield?" Matthew inquired.

The man answered, "Yer doctors an medical supply people should have what ya need."

"We don't see them," the teen explained.

"Ya kin have some a what I have an I'll git more from the hospital tamorra when I'm there. Come on it."

They entered the house and the door was closed behind them. The first thing they noticed was the warmth. It had been weeks since the two had been inside a building, especially one with some heat.

"I wish we didn't hav ta go back outside," Blake whispered.

"This is nice," the other remarked.

Doctor Darlington led them into his office. Realizing they were deadly serious about wanting to help wounded soldiers, he sat them down to explain things to them.

"I admire yer wish ta he'p an wan'ta explain some thins to ya." Calling out to his son he asked, "Johnny, bring me a large flour sack from the kitchen." Turning back to the boys he continued, "I'll give ya some thins an explain them." Reaching into a cabinet he pulled out several items. "These are rolls a bandages. Ya kin do lots with them." Picking up a pair of thin boards he went on. "These are splints. Ya kin use bandages ta tie them to a broken arm or leg ta keep it tagether." Picking up a mid sized tin he continued. "This is alum. It's a styptic. Thet means it he'ps blood ta clot. When someone has a wound thet bleeds a lot, ya use it ta stop the bleedin. Ya kin also use a bandage an one a these sticks if ya have a bad bleedin wound on a arm 'r leg, an make a tourniquet."

"I seen thet once," Blake cut in.

Johnny returned with the bag.

"I'll put these in this bag an ya kin put it in yer hav'sack fer when ya might need it. Here's extras." The doctor took more from his supplies in the cabinet.

"Good luck ta ya an stay alive."

The man walked them to the door. They waved back as they started up the street, then turned back toward the camp.

* * *

Christmas came the following week. With the help of the musicians the men sang some Christmas carols. It snowed some. On the following day, the general gave orders to move out. The army was headed for Murfreesboro. Battle with the Confederate army was at hand.

* * *

On Christmas Day evening a heavy rain began to fall, continuing through the night. Friday morning, December 26th, dawned cold and grey. The long roll echoed throughout Nashville and the surrounding countryside. The soldiers took up arms leaving their tents and personal gear behind. Canteens were filled and some had the barest of utensils and a tin cup. Blake and Matthew had divided their medical supplies between them and packed them in their haversacks. They were issued three days rations which they carried in their haversacks, and carried thirty rounds of ammunition in their cartridge boxes. Drum rolls were traded for cadences and the air filled with the shouts of orders, the tramp of thousands of feet, the calls of bugles, the jingle of trace chains with the movement of horses, artillery, and wagons. The 31st, within the 2nd of the divisions commanded by General Crittenden, left Nashville by way of the Nashville Pike, traveling southeast toward Murfreesboro. They were the left wing of the army, which had been divided into three parts, each traveling by a different set of roads. The army was on the road, leaving Nashville behind, by six o'clock in the morning.

The musicians stayed with the companies to keep a cadence for the march. They stayed to the front by the captain and played a number of lively march pieces with periods of drum cadence in between. Blake marched beside them to serve as courier or backup musician as needed. He carried his rifle because he had it. All the musicians had were their musician's swords. Their hands were occupied with their music. There was no conversation. They needed to keep quiet and pay attention to orders as they came down, and besides, they hadn't the energy for it. The predominant sound was the rhythmic marching of eighteen thousand pairs of feet stretched out over miles of highway.

It was around seven o'clock when the front of the column came in contact with outposts of Confederate cavalry. After brief skirmishing, the army moved on. Later in the day the front was again deployed for battle. Wheeler's entire cavalry brigade confronted them. As the men of the 31st waited, they could hear the sounds of battle to the front. The army's advance was continually interrupted over the next two days as it was repeatedly harassed by enemy cavalry. Finally, in the late afternoon gloom of the 29th, the corps approached Stones River which followed along the left of the roadway for a little more than a half mile before crossing over in the front. Beyond the river by another half mile lay Murfreesboro. To the right of the roadway lay dense thickets of cedar trees.

Blake's company followed the rest of the regiment as they moved off the right side of the road and tramped their way into the cedar thickets. The rocky terrain sloped downhill in front of them toward the river below. The rest of the division spread out in line of battle on either side, two columns deep, with artillery batteries deployed on either side of the brigade.

"Look!" Beverly whispered pointing to their front. "Their whole damn army's down there!"

"But somebody said they were retreating!" Christopher exclaimed.

"Thet ain't no retreat," Blake added.

To the far left a Union brigade splashed across the river and advanced against the Confederates. The boys watched in horror as gunfire echoed in the hills and the single brigade advanced, forcing enemy pickets to retreat, over nearly five hundred yards. They then came up against the entire enemy division and were forced in turn to retreat. The action ended.

As night approached, the order went out that there would be no fires. They could give the enemy artillery targets and cost many lives. Rain set in. The boys lay down on the wet ground for the night, suffering in the downpour and the mud.

Over the next day, the generals played chess with their armies as they moved some of their divisions from place to place. General Palmer's division stayed in its place and the men of the 31st became spectators as they watched out across fields and wood lots, waiting for the inevitable. They had a good view. The regiment had been placed in the front line along with the 2nd Kentucky, with the cedar woods to their back. Sounds of scattered gunfire could be heard throughout the day as Confederate skirmishers and sharpshooters harassed the Union movements. Darkness deepened. Sometime before tattoo, a Federal band struck up a rendition of "Yankee Doodle" followed by "Hail Columbia." After a few more popular tunes, the band yielded as a Confederate band opened with a series of Southern favorites. The exchanges continued for a while, then the Federal band began "Home Sweet Home" and was immediately joined by the Confederate band. One by one more bands took up the tune until the bands throughout both armies were playing together.

Blake was struck with emotion as he thought of home for the first time in weeks. What had his family done when they found he was missing? What did they think had happened? Tears flowed quietly. He observed that all along the line tears were flowing in shameless abundance as men tried to sing along.

The music ceased, the refrain of the song drifting to silence in the cool frosty air.

* * *

Shortly after six o'clock on the last morning of the year, sounds of battle drifted in from the far right. The onslaught had begun.

"It's started," Matthew stated.

"Enythin in front?" Blake asked.

"Hold steady, Men," Captain Ristine whispered. "Stay alert for any movement from the enemy."

The thud of artillery and the roar of infantry grew more intense from the far right. After an hour battle erupted again to the right, but much closer. A rumbling sound of heavy wagons approached from the right accompanied by a sound like a big wind preceding a big storm, and gradually intensified.

"Something's happened," John stated nervously.

"Look behind, in the trees!" Timothy exclaimed.

"There's cannon being pulled by their crews, horses without riders, men bloodied and wounded; some have their guns and some don't!" Beverly observed.

"Listen!" Blake added. "The yells a the enemy!"

John concluded, "I think the divisions on the far right have been whipped and are in full retreat."

"We best look sharp," Matthew advised.

The retreating soldiers continued to pour through the woods behind the line. There were men helping wounded comrades, many with faces blacked by powder and covered with blood. There were empty wagons pulled by runaway teams. For nearly an hour the thousands retreated across the back of the division's battle line.

As ten o'clock neared and movement was observed in the opposing Confederate line, General Cruft, brigade commander, ordered his skirmishers forward.

As the skirmishers moved forward, one of the officers observed, "Before they come after us, why don't we use the rocks about us and build a stone wall?"

"Good idea," Christopher agreed. He unstrapped his drum and began to pick up rocks to line up in the front of the regiment's position. Soon the men of the various companies laid their guns on the ground and joined in gathering stones for the wall. Impressively, a strong wall took shape.

"Some a ya he'p me take this fence down so ar people kin come back fast an the enemy doesn't have nothing ta hide b'hind." Blake stepped forward and began to dismantle the rail fence in front of the wall. As the wall took shape by the hands of many, others went forward to help destroy the rail fence.

"They're coming!" Lieutenant Kidner shouted.

"Wait for our men to cross, then fire on my command," Captain Ristine ordered.

The yells of the enemy pierced the air as the skirmishers cleared the wall, followed by a half dozen regiments of enemy soldiers.

"Fire!" The command was given all up and down the wall.

Muskets roared as flame and lead shot forth in massive force. The wall of lead slammed into the attacking mass and a fearful slaughter of grey-clad men and boys fell on the slope in front. Return fire was minimum as the Confederates fell back and the regiment reloaded. Again the enemy charged and again the wall of flame and lead met their advance, and the dead and wounded fell in piles. The brigade's regiments had been destroyed. As the remnants struggled to fall back, another brigade with its five regiments advanced in steady step. Once more the line of guns roared. Torn flesh and blood filled the air as bodies were shattered and more fell on the tops of the piles that had fallen before.

As some defenders of the wall fell dead or wounded, Timothy began to help wounded to the rear while the remaining musicians took up their cartridge and cap boxes and rifles and fired on the enemy. Blake could see that Matthew was having a hard time, trying to help the wounded, but coming dangerously close to becoming one himself.

"Tyler told me ta think a them as ragin bears who would kill me if I didn't shoot them," Blake advised. "An I knew he were right if I didn't wanna die. So I did."

"Thanks," Matthew acknowledged. He took up a rifle and fired at the nearest enemy soldier. He missed.

As the soldier fired back, Blake kicked his friend aside. Someone else fired on the soldier and he went down. The two boys reloaded and continued the fight.

The 31st and the 2nd Kentucky having nearly exhausted their cartridge supply, the second line was sent forward to relieve them as still another enemy charge approached. As the relief regiments approached, their colonel ordered a charge.

"Down!" The order ran the line.

The men of the 31st lay down and the men of the 1st Kentucky went over them, advancing beyond the wall. Running into a crossfire of musketry and artillery, they fell back. Again they charged over the 31st, followed by double lines of the enemy.

"Fire in line!" the captain ordered.

Again the guns along the line roared with such a deadly volley that the enemy rapidly retreated. Still the Confederates attacked. until the

Union line ran low on ammunition and was forced to fall back.

Christopher grabbed his drum as the regiment withdrew from their place at the wall. Matthew paused to help a wounded comrade to the rear. Some remained at the wall to cover the brigade's withdrawal. The enemy fired on them. Those at the wall fired back and again the enemy paused. Matthew went down.

"Where ar ya hit?" Blake asked, rushing to his side.

"Knocked my leg right out from under me."

Blake knelt to examine the wound and saw a large hole torn through the muscle of his lower left leg with blood flowing rapidly, soaking Matthew's pants. He remembered Steven's accident and Jackson's tourniquet.

"Pull yer leg up with yer hands," he instructed as he pulled a bandage and a splint from his haversack.

As Matthew steadied his leg, the boy quickly wrapped a bandage below the knee, tied the end of the splint into the knot, then twisted the stick until the bleeding stopped. "Hold this." He put Matthew's hand on the end of the stick while he pulled out another bandage and tied the stick in place.

The wounded soldier whom Matthew had been helping had watched, fascinated, as Blake had tended Matthew's wound.

"What did you do?" the soldier asked.

"It's a turnicut," he answered, "We gotta git outa here. Kin ya walk?"

"I think so." Matthew struggled to his feet. "Not broken," he observed. Suddenly he became light headed and grabbed Blake for balance. "I don't feel too good." He started to slip to the ground.

"Kin ya he'p me?" Blake asked the soldier.

He, too, struggled to his feet. His left arm hung useless at his side. "I think I can walk. Can't do much else." Nevertheless, he reached out with his good arm and helped keep Matthew from falling to the ground.

The battle continued along the stone wall. The boys were struggling about thirty yards behind the conflict as they tried to move off to a safe position.

"Here, carry this." Blake handed Matthew's musket to the wounded soldier. He slung his own over his shoulder and tried to get a grip on Matthew in order to help him to safety.

More soldiers who were running out of ammunition, passed to the rear. "Let me help," one offered. He stooped down and wrapped his arms around the older boy's legs and lifted him over his shoulder. Blake took his friend's gun back from the wounded soldier and walked beside him as the four worked their way toward the rear.

* * *

Matthew and the wounded soldier were left with a surgeon and his assistants at a hospital site along the Nashville Pike. Blake found his way back to the regiment, now to the right of the pike where new lines had been drawn up beside a round, forested hill. There was a lull in the fighting. The enemy could be seen in the distance realigning its army. The Union army was using the opportunity to bring in extra artillery and position it on the hill.

"Where are Matthew and Christopher?" Beverly asked as the younger boy returned to his position with the musicians.

"Matthew's with the hospital folk up the pike." Blake was worried. "I thought Christopher was with ya all. I saw him pick up his drum an musket and leave with ya."

"Not here," John confirmed. "When we're done here, we'll go look for him."

During the lull of the afternoon, Confederate artillery kept firing on the hill. All watched as the Confederate infantry crossed the Stones River and formed a line of attack with two brigades.

"Here they come," Lieutenant Kidner whispered.

"Hold your fire," the brigade's General Cruft ordered.

As the eight hundred enemy approached, their lines were torn apart by artillery. Once in range, the order was given to fire.

The sheet of flame and lead roared forth and the enemy fell in large numbers. They quickly retreated. Even as they left the field, two more brigades could be seen forming up.

"Cain't they see as it's hopeless?" Blake wondered aloud.

"They're crazy," Timothy added.

Minutes later, the second charge was destroyed. The day's fighting came to a close.

* * *

As twilight faded to dark, the artillery ceased and sporadic gunfire faded to an occasional popping. A cold rain fell and fires were lit to try and provide some warmth. There was little to eat. The supply trains had been disrupted by Confederate cavalry. Temperatures fell to freezing.

"Bradford," Beverly said, "I want to check on Matthew then try to find Christopher."

"I'll take us ta Matthew. Then we kin folla the way back ta where we last saw Christopher."

Blake led the way to the hospital area and looked around until he found where their friend lay in the rainfall on the wet ground. He seemed asleep.

"Matthew," Beverly asked, "are you awake?"

The youth opened his eyes and pushed himself into a seated position. His pant leg was ripped open and the wound had been bandaged.

"The doctor said as you saved my life. Still, I lost a lot of blood."

"Kin ya leave here?" Blake asked.

"Not yet. They're going to send me back to the hospital in Nashville."

"I wanna go with ya. Try ta stay here a while. We's gonna try ta find Christopher. He's missin."

"Be careful." Matthew sounded worried.

"We will," Beverly assured.

The boys worked their way across the roadway toward the cedar woods. At first they had the light from the campfires to help them see their way. Once in the woods, they had to feel their way from tree to tree, using the fires to orient them. It was slow going. All around were the moans of the wounded who had tried to make their way back for help or who had been struck down during the retreat. Some called for help, for a fire, for water, for their mothers, for God's help to end their suffering. It was all the boys could do to continue on without stopping to help ease the suffering all around them. Beverly tripped over something and fell, landing on a mound of fabric. Blake helped him up and they checked to see what was there. As Blake ran his hands over the obstacle on the ground, he felt something sticky, with fabric frozen stiff.

"Oh, God," he got sick and vomited without warning. "They's piles a dead froze in ther own blood an gore!"

The thought of it turned Beverly's stomach and he grabbed a tree as he, too, got sick.

"We have to go on," he said choking and coughing and spitting out his vomit. He wiped his face with his sleeve.

They moved on slowly, carefully picking their way among the piles of dead, made all the more slippery by the continuing rain on the blood-soaked ground.

"We must be past our lines." The youth paused holding onto a tree. "These piles of dead would be in front of our line, not behind it."

Using the sounds of the camp, the two worked back toward the pike. Blake banged up against something and nearly fell over the stone wall.

"I think this is it," he observed.

"Let's start back up the hill." Beverly took the younger boy's arm as they carefully crossed the stonework.

They had gone but a few steps when Blake announced, "Bev, I think I found something." He bent down. "It's a drum."

The moans of the wounded filled the landscape.

"Christopher," Beverly called.

"Are ya here, Christopher," Blake added.

Something stirred. The boys moved toward the noise. Suddenly, a hand wrapped around Blake's ankle.

"Help!" he screamed.

Beverly rushed over to the shadow that was his friend and took his arm. "What is it?"

"Somthin grabbed ma foot."

Getting down on his hands and knees to crawl among the bodies, the young teen checked closely to try and see what was at Blake's feet. He heard a heavy sigh and strained his eyes to see more clearly. Putting his hands on the body, he felt it move. Sliding his hands across the chest, he felt the drum strap and he felt a sticky mass of wool.

"I think it's Christopher. I feel a drum strap and he's bin shot. I felt the blood."

"How kin we git him outta here?" Blake cried in frustration.

"We'll have to try and carry him as best we can."

"Should I bring his drum?"

"You can try if you want."

Carefully Blake removed the drum strap and rehooked it over his shoulders, careful not to tangle it with his rifle. He crawled to find the drum and clipped it to the strap sliding it toward his back. The two then tried to take Christopher by his arms and lift him from the ground. With a great deal of effort, they began to drag him through the woods toward the sounds of the army's camps. The drummer hung limp as dead weight, drifting in and out of consciousness, as his sword bounced and clicked over bodies, rocks, and other objects littering the ground.

An hour later, the three broke through the edge of the cedars and into the firelight of the camps. They worked their way to the hospital area and gently lay their burden on the wet ground, rainfall dancing off his face. They were all thoroughly soaked by the rain, but too busy with Christopher to notice. An officer in a white coat approached.

Kneeling to check for wounds he announced, "You needn't have bothered to bring him in. He's dead – in five minutes or five hours, it's still the same. The bullet went through his lung." He left.

"He ain't dead yet. Let's git him ta Matthew."

The two took their drummer friend, found Matthew, and placed him by the older boy's side.

In the dim light of the fires, they could see that Christopher was conscious. Under his jacket, his chest was covered in blood, still bubbling out of the bullet hole.

"I'll be right back," Beverly announced. "I'm going to tell the captain." He ran off to tell the news.

Timothy returned with the bugler and together they sat with their friend through the night, freezing as they huddled in the rain.

As the first day of the new year dawned and the cold rains of the night ended, Timothy held his friend's hand and felt it relax as the drummer breathed his last.

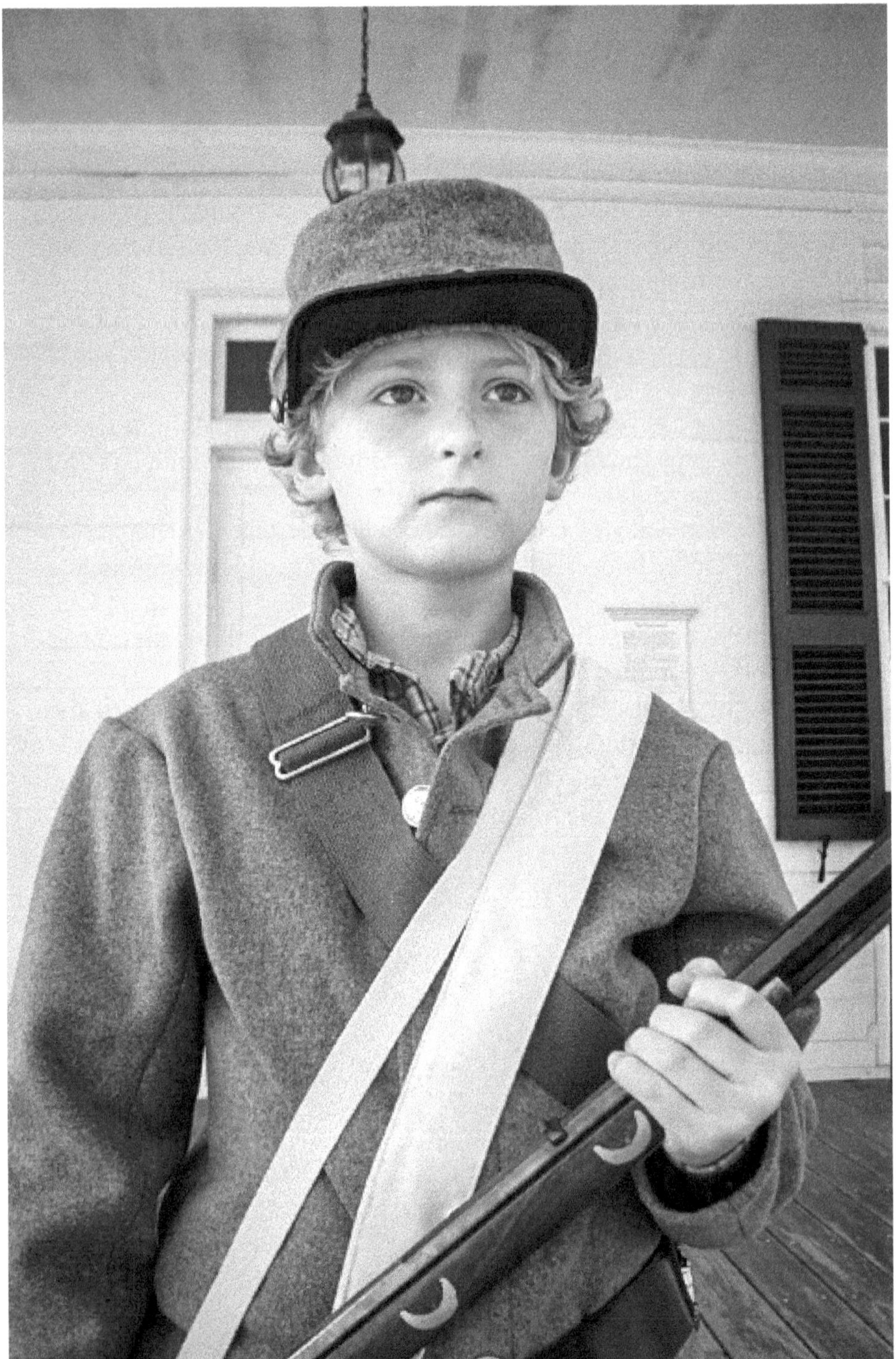

Chapter Six
The Return Home

Lieutenant Kidner was devastated by Christopher's death. During the quiet of New Year's Day, he got permission from the captain to take the body for burial to the stone wall. All his personal gear was stowed in his haversack and placed with his sword and drum on the ground where the musicians slept. Dressed in the uniform in which he died and wrapped in a blanket, Christopher was laid to rest by the officer and his closest friends. Stones were taken from the wall to mark and cover the grave to prevent wild animals from being able to disturb it. Matthew was absent. He had been taken back to Nashville in one of the ambulance trains.

The 31st was involved in one final action in the late afternoon of the 2nd amid rain and sleet. Then it was over. The weather let up briefly before continuing after dark. During the following day the Confederate Army began to withdraw toward Shelbyville and Manchester and eventually to Tullahoma. The Union Army withdrew to Nashville. The 31st along with its brigade, however, moved eight miles east of Murfreesboro and went into camp at Cripple Creek. As the new drummer for the company, Blake was given Christopher's sword and drum and proudly joined the musicians for the march, cloaked in an air of sadness for those who were lost or left behind.

"Private, sound assembly." Blake picked up the drum sticks, strapped on Christopher's drum and struck the call.

The company gathered in the predawn light of the new day and awaited the captain's instructions.

"Today," Captain Ristine began, "we are assigned to guard the train of wagons to come back from Nashville and bring back our camp, personal gear, and provisions for the brigade. We leave right after breakfast."

The company was dismissed to stir up their fires and prepare a breakfast of hard bread, bacon, and coffee. Once again, they had no packs, only the clothes on their backs and the contents of their haversacks. Once again, ramrods and swords did duty as cooking utensils.

"Lieutenant," Blake asked, wandering to the officer's fire with his coffee, "kin we find Matthew when wer in Nashville an bring him back with us?"

"I will give you, Beverly, and Timothy written orders to take him from whatever hospital you find him in and return him to the company." He poured another cup of coffee, then stood to face the boy once more. "But first, you must get ready for the march."

"Yes, Sir," the boy replied. He returned to his fire and told the others.

A light snow had begun with the dawn and continued to accumulate on the landscape, turning the world white. The entire regiment was assigned to train guard duty to ensure a large enough force to discourage Confederate harassment. All would join together for the march to Nashville where the wagons waited.

"Private, sound assembly," Sergeant Carson ordered.

The drum rolled as others throughout the regiment took up the call. The troops assembled, armed for battle if need be, carrying three days rations from the meager supplies in the few wagons that managed to accompany the brigade from Murfreesboro, which should get them through the march, expected to last but two days.

"Private Sanderson," the lieutenant addressed the fifer, "as senior musician, here are your orders for the musicians to recover Private Mills from the hospital." He handed the paper to Timothy who in turn filed it inside his coat.

"Thank you, Sir," he acknowledged.

The company was in line to depart. Drums sounded the cadence as the 31st formed up. The Field Music assembled at the front. The command was given. The lead drummer and fifer began the march, followed in short order by the massed musicians. The regiment headed west in parade formation, drifting off through the falling snow.

* * *

Late in the day, a company of Confederate cavalry was seen in the distance, but they left the marching column alone. That night the 31st bivouacked just east of Lavergne, entering their old camps in the late afternoon of the second day. Finally, they could receive rations for coffee, meat, and bread and sleep in tents with blankets. The musicians were called to the captain's fire.

The Return Home

Captain Ristine spoke, "The lieutenant has given private Sanderson orders to find and return Private Mills." He finished his coffee and picked up the steaming pot for a refill. Placing it back on the fire, he continued. "We will remain in camp tomorrow as our companies pick up wagons from the wagon park and load provisions from Taylor Depot at the railroad terminal. The wagon train will be assembled on the open fields at brigade headquarters. The following morning we pack the camps and start back. You have tomorrow to search the hospitals and find the private. Any questions as you carry out your orders, see the lieutenant. You're dismissed."

"Yes, Sir." The three saluted. He returned the salute then turned to his desk to work on paperwork.

"Lieutenant, Sir?" Blake asked, "whar da we start?"

The officer walked with them toward their fire. "You might start with your doctor friend and see what help he can offer."

"Thank you, Sir." Timothy turned to their fire and poured a cup of coffee.

The three sat around their fire as the man left. John joined them. "Any news?" he asked.

"Not yet," Timothy answered, "we'll let you know tomorrow."

Blake had been assigned into the musicians' tent. Rather than stay alone, John crowed in with them.

"Private, sound tattoo," the sergeant ordered.

The drummer called the camp to their tents as he struck tattoo to allow fifteen minutes before taps. The camp began to settle. Taps echoed through the darkness as the black of night closed over the site.

* * *

Blake led the way as the party left the camp and headed toward the doctor's house. As always, he carried rifle, cartridge box and cap box, with canteen and haversack slung over his shoulder. The other two carried canteen and haversack. Pedestrian traffic was light, mostly women and children. As the boys turned down the street toward the Darlington house, Jimmy and a friend greeted them from the other side, his arm still in its sling.

"Wait!" he called as the two dashed across the street to meet them. "Ya bin gone mor'n a week. What happened?"

"Ya herd ther was a fight?" Blake began.

"Ever'one talked 'bout it," Jimmy replied. "Wher ya goin?"

"Going to see Doctor Darlington to find out how to find someone in the hospitals," Beverly explained.

"Who's hurt?" Jimmy's friend asked.

"Matthew was wounded in the fighting and they brought him back here in the ambulance train," Timothy responded.

"Christopher's dead," Blake announced quietly.

"Sorry," Jimmy said. "I really got ta like him."

They were at the doctor's. The three turned in at the gate as the other two paused. Jimmy whispered to his friend who turned quietly and left.

"I'm goin with ya," the boy announced. "I kin he'p ya find the hospit'ls."

The door opened and Doctor Darlington stepped out with medical bag in hand.

Seeing the boys he asked, "What brings ya boys here taday? Haven't seen ya fer days." He approached the front gate. "Ya in thet fightin on New Years?"

The boys waited at the fence.

"Yes, Sir," Timothy volunteered. "We're trying to find Matthew somewhere in these hospitals."

"Walk with me ta the Planters Hotel where I have ta check on some officer patients an I'll 'splain 'long the way how ta look. If enyone asks questions, ya says ta see me, Doctor Marcus Darlington, if they has concerns. "I see Jimmy's with ya. He knows his way 'round an 'll be a big he'p."

The doctor went on to explain that there's usually a clerk of record keeping at every hospital who has the names of all the patients in a book. But there are over two dozen hospitals and that will take a lot of looking. Pointing to a three-story brick building with a higher clock tower several blocks away, he informed, "Thet's Howard school. Thet's one hospital with at least two hundred and fifty patients. The Union Hospital No. 19 is off toward the south. If yer a volunteer regiment, ya might look thar."

They had arrived at the three-story Planters Hotel with street-side balconies on each floor.

"Thanks, Doctor," Sanderson said. "We'll follow Jimmy here and ask about to find the hospitals and see the clerk when we find one." As the boys left, the doctor turned toward the hotel's porch.

Jimmy and his friends wandered the snow-covered packed dirt streets in search of the hospitals. They were crowded with people, some dressed like businessmen and many blacks and laborers. Some appeared friendly and some looked dangerous. Finding their first hospital, the fifer found the clerk, showed him his orders, and asked about Private Mills. He wasn't there. They moved on. They were struck with the activity in the yard of one hospital as it was crowded with volunteers and former slaves hanging out bed linens and hospital gowns on a crisscross of lines to dry in the open air. In general, they hung limp in the cold air and some froze like hanging white boards.

They had entered their ninth hospital and watched as the clerk went through the list of names. He paused and looked back over the written order Timothy had handed him.

"Here's a Private Matthew Mills age eighteen, listed with a wound to the leg."

"Kin we see him?" Blake asked.

"Says here he's on the second floor a buildin four. Thet's the house o'er ther," he pointed. "Find him an bring him back here an I kin take him off ma list."

The four dashed through the laundry hanging throughout the yard as they crossed to building four. Once inside, they worked their way through the stench of urine and filthy bodies and dimly lit hallways, peering into rooms along the way in search of their friend. An assortment of wounded moved or lay about the building. Some with bandages walked about and some just sat on a chair or in a bed in a stuporous daze. There were many with missing arms or legs or hands or feet. Some moved about in crude wheel chairs or with crutches, or stayed seated or lying down on some surface.

"Have ya seen Private Matthew Mills?" they asked over and over of anyone who would pay any attention. Finally a black girl carrying a pile of sheets responded.

"He a skinny little man, little taller then uze?"

"Yes," Timothy responded.

"He goes round wid the docterin folk an he'ps ten ta the hurtin folk."

"Thet's him," Blake burst with excitement. "Whar is he?"

"The kitch'n in the big house." She pointed to the main building where the clerk's office was located.

"Thanks." Blake hurried toward the stairway.

The other three followed as they rushed back to the main building to find the kitchen.

"Where's the kitchen?" Timothy asked the clerk as they burst into his office.

"End a the main hall."

The three musicians and friend rushed down the hall and stormed into the kitchen.

"Matthew!" they shouted.

Matthew turned from the cook stove. "God am I glad to see you!" He rushed into the open arms of his friends.

"Jimmy! You're here, too!" He broke away from the others and gave the small boy a gentle hug. "Thanks."

A large black woman, an ex-slave, looked up from the table where she was cutting potatoes for a stew.

"Land sakes! What's this all 'bout!"

"He's from our company," Timothy explained. "We have orders to find him and bring him back." He held the paper for the woman to see.

"We gotta go," Blake announced. "The clerk said he has ta check 'im out."

"Bye, Sally," Matthew waved to the cook.

"Ya be good," she waved back. "'N don't go gittin shot agin."

The five found the clerk. He took note of the orders and signed Matthew out of the log book.

Daylight was fading as the four young soldiers and young friend worked their way back through the city toward their camps.

"I had heard the regiment didn't come back and was worried I had lost you for good." Matthew walked with a slight limp as he worked to keep up with the musicians.

"We wasn't sher ta be able ta find ya," Blake admitted. "But Docter Darlin'ton told us how an Jimmy he'p ta find ar way 'round."

"How's your leg?" Timothy asked as they trudged along in the snow.

"It's getting pretty good," the older teen answered. "The surgeon said the bullet went through without hitting the bone, but tore a big hole in everything else. I'd have bled to death if it hadn't been for the tourniquet. He sewed it all back together and put a bandage on it and took off the tourniquet. It still oozes and the thread's still in it. The regiment's doctor can check on it and cut them out when it's time."

The Return Home

As the four turned off the main road onto a side street near a section of houses, they noticed a pair of dark shadows that seemed to be moving in the bushes beside them. Blake glanced at Matthew and nodded ever so slightly.

"Cum on little broth'r," he took Jimmy's left arm. "We gotta git home now. Ar fo'ks is gonna wunder whar we is." The two turned away from the shadows, a surprised look on Jimmy's face, and walked back to a nearby house. Blake whispered into Jimmy's ear and all was understood.

"What the…!" Beverly was cut off.

"It's okay. They had to go," Matthew said.

The shadows moved ahead. Suddenly two dirty-looking men in their early twenties dashed out into the road in front with muskets pointing at the boys.

"They's two a us as jest left?" one asked.

Matthew responded, "He's just a local friend and his brother who likes to dress up and play soldier. He doesn't even have a regular gun."

"Well we's gonna make sum money. Yer goin wi us ta the local malitia."

The two stepped forward to prod the boys with their guns, fearless seeing none of the boys was armed. One had his musket at Timothy's ribs and the other near Matthew's waist. Suddenly, a shot rang out and the one near Timothy dropped and the one near Matthew looked to see what happened. A piercing yell came from the trees as Timothy grabbed the rifle from the ground at his feet and Matthew yanked the rifle from the hands of the stranger beside him.

"What the Hell!" the one standing exclaimed.

"Like I said," Matthew explained, "he may be a Reb, but he's our friend. He's also a soldier from the war. His brother is really a friend of ours from the area."

"What do we do now?" Timothy asked.

"They can't do much harm now," Matthew replied. He spoke to the man standing, "We're taking your muskets, cartridges, and caps. You take your friend and get him help."

Blake and Jimmy returned from their place in the trees and the older boy stopped to reload his rifle. Beverly and Timothy collected the guns and ammunition.

"Ya was so calm!" Jimmy exclaimed. "Ya jest aimed and shot like a 'sperienced hunter!"

The man on the ground asked, "Why don't ya shoot us? Ya got ar loaded guns."

"We ain't her ta kill no'ne," Blake explained. "In battle, if som'ne is comin ta kill us, we do as we has ta stay 'live. We ain't wantin ta hurt ya none." He picked up his gun and slung it back over his shoulder.

"Yer lucky," Jimmy added. "These soldiers ain't killers."

"Let's go," Timothy said.

The five left the would-be bounty hunters behind and continued on toward camp as Jimmy waved good-bye and turned toward home.

* * *

"Too bad they didn't kill you," Sergeant Carson sneered as the boys returned to camp and he stepped close to Matthew's ear. "You're no soldier. You're a disgrace. Can't even shoot the enemy."

"Leave it alone, Sergeant," Lieutenant Kidner ordered. Turning to the boys he continued, "Private Timmons has your rations. Fix your dinner before it's too dark." To Matthew he added, "It's good to have you back, Private Mills."

The youth smiled in appreciation as the four walked to their campfire and found John and their food for dinner.

* * *

Monday the 11th dawned cold and grey. The brigade's camps were struck and loaded onto the extra wagons gathered for each regiment's camp, equipment, and personal gear. By midmorning the train was ready to start back to Cripple Creek.

Jimmy stopped to watch as the wagons were loaded. He knew he would never see these friends again and hated to see them go. Each, in turn gave him a gentle hug and a salute fare well. Blake put his pack down and pulled out his drum sticks and strap from within.

"Jimmy, we nev'r did git yer ful name."

"It's James Connor Dickson."

"Well James Connor Dickson, these ar mine I brung from home. I want ya ta have em. I have Christopher's an they mean a lot ta me." He handed them to his young friend.

"Thanks," was all Jimmy could manage. He smiled in appreciation of this special treasure he had just received, then grabbed his friend in a last hug, as tight as his good arm would allow, receiving a strong, but gentle, hug in return. Standing back with tears in his eyes he offered, "Be kerful. Yer ma friends."

He stood and watched for as long as it took for the wagon train to depart, then turned sadly in the empty quiet to walk home.

* * *

Train guard duty meant that the regiment would be spread out for about a half mile, the length of the supply train's hundred wagons. It was a long and difficult trip. The soldiers had to march as best they could along either side of the pike. The day to day weather varied from snow to sleet to freezing rain. Roads turned muddy. Often wagons bogged down in the mud and groups of men would have to put their shoulders to the wheels and push them free. Some wagons broke down as an axle snapped or a wheel gave way. Skilled craftsmen from a company could take a broken axle to a nearby barn for the night and by morning, have a new one. Broken wheels seemed to get passed around. The teamsters from the wagon with the broken wheel waited by the side of the road for someone to leave a good wagon unattended. It was a simple matter to prop up the good wagon for just a moment in order to swap the broken wheel for a good one. In this manner a single broken wheel seemed to find its way to a number of wagons in turn. Eventually, the train would pass by a farm with a good wagon and the broken wheel would finally leave the train. Near the end of the week the train finally arrived at the brigade's camps and the regiments recovered their tents, gear, and equipment, and winter camp was established.

* * *

January slipped into February. The surgeon removed the stitching from Matthew's leg. The camp routine carried on in a mix of chores – firewood gathering, hunting, foraging about the countryside, and drill and monotony. Blake's days followed from drum call to drum call, from reveille to taps.

"Lieutenant," Blake began after breakfast the first day of February, "Ya said way back as ya'd he'p me git back ta ma army."

"I did," he acknowledged. "But things have gone along in such a routine that I had forgotten and just taken it for granted that you were now one of us."

"Ya all bin real good ta me an I feel a part a the 31st. But I cam in ta this war ta kill Yanks, caus one killed my father at Shiloh, an I don wanna kill eny'ne eny more. I jest wanna go home." The boy stood before the officer, filled with a sadness that was almost overwhelming.

"I was at Shiloh. The slaughter there was as bad as Stones River," the officer reflected.

"Where was ya ther?" Blake asked.

"The regiment fought with General Prentiss and others at a ridge that was nicknamed the hornet's nest, because there was such an intense firing of bullets that they seemed like a swarm of hornets."

Blake was thunderstruck by the information. "Is thet wher Matthew killed the Confederate thet made him sick?"

"Yes. Sit down by the fire, Bradford. Have some hot coffee."

The boy did as the man said and the officer sat on his camp stool beside him. Both starred into the flames and were absorbed by their crackling sound.

"I can't very well let you just up and walk off into the countryside. Your home is hundreds of miles from here and it's not likely you would survive the journey." He sat in silence, caught in the dilemma. "Your army is camped at Tullahoma. That's about fifty miles from here. In good weather you might walk it in three days. It's still the dead of winter. I'll think on it and talk to the captain."

"Thank ya, Sir." The boy finished his coffee, put the cup on the ground beside the fire, then stood to leave.

He walked back to his tent with his head spinning in torment. Oh, God, he thought, it could have been Matthew who killed his father. But Matthew was like a brother. He couldn't hate him. His heart ached – for the loss of his father and for the deep pain it had brought to Matthew. He had lost a father for whom he held such a deep love and whose death had brought such deep pain. Now he found that that death had brought such deep pain to another for whom he cared so much.

Blake sat down by his fire, lost in a hurt that sucked the air out of his chest leaving a painful vacuum that wanted to collapse his lungs.

Matthew glanced over from where he sat at his tent and saw the pain on Blake's face, unlike any pain he had ever seen in another. He stood and walked to his friend's side and settled on the log beside him.

"What's wrong," he asked in alarm.

But the boy couldn't say anything. He stared at the flames in silence until suddenly, he burst into uncontrollable tears. Matthew reached out toward him and Blake wrapped his arms around his friend, buried his face in his coat and cried his heart out. No words were spoken. Matthew was suddenly torn by his young friend's grief and found himself lost to tears. They sat together, huddled in a deep sadness, momentarily beyond their control.

Again Matthew asked, "Bradford, what's wrong?"

"I wanna go home. I hate this war an jest wanna go home."

"If I could take you home, I would," Matthew cried, still fighting to control his own tears.

The musicians returned with John, each with an armful of firewood. They dropped their loads by the fire and were taken by surprise by the deep grief evident before them. Looking at each other, they were lost for words.

"What's wrong?" Timothy asked.

Matthew shook his head. "Bradford's hurting something fierce and I don't know why." He looked at his friends as a tear slipped free from his eyes. "He's crying uncontrollably and just wants to go home. I don't know what to do," he struggled to control his voice. "I want to help, but just don't know what to do."

John went to get the lieutenant. The officer came quickly.

"What happened," Kidner asked.

"I don't know," Matthew replied. "He was sitting here starring into the fire. I came over to ask what was wrong and he just started crying and saying he wanted to go home."

"He had come to me to say he wanted to go back to his army, then that he wanted to go home," the man shared. "He said how his father was killed at Shiloh and he came to the war to kill Yanks, but he doesn't want to do that any more. I told him how we were at Shiloh with Prentiss and he got real quiet."

Matthew guessed he knew what was wrong. "Sir, if there is any way to do it, I want to take Bradford home. He doesn't belong here any more than I do. If there is any way to make it safe, I can take him to his army at Tullahoma and get safe passage most of the way by train."

Blake started to settle down as he listened to the request. As he did, Matthew, too, was able to regain control of his emotions and relax.

"I will talk to the captain," Lieutenant Kidner decided.

* * *

Friday morning dawned with an overcast sky trying to thin and let the sun shine through. Matthew had his full pack including half of a dog tent, as well as his musket and all his gear. Blake was back in his Confederate uniform, but with Christopher's sword at his side, and fully packed the same as Matthew. Christopher's drum sticks and strap were carefully tucked inside the pack. Blake carried the drum slung over his shoulder. A coffee pot hung from the bottom of Mathew's pack. They walked west toward Murfreesboro where the railroad ran southeast to Tullahoma. There was no train traffic because the Union Army was at one end and the Confederate at the other.

Matthew carried a set of orders that Captain Ristine had worked out with Brigadeer General Charles Cruft, the brigade commander. Private Matthew Mills was promoted to Corporal and detached from the army on special assignment to escort Private Bradford James of the Confederate Army back to his home in Shelby, North Carolina. Upon completion of his assignment he was discharged from the army for medical reasons resulting from injuries in battle. He was to be guaranteed safe passage in discharging his assignment, expected to be honored by both armies and upheld by their general officers. They were signed by Captain Andrew Ristine, company commander, and Brigadeer General Charles Cruft, brigade commander.

The first night was spent in a farm yard on the edge of Murfreesboro within sight of the railroad, well away from any part of the battlefield. Buttoning the tent halves together, they pitched the tent using pieces of tree branches scattered on the ground. The drum and sword were placed safely in the back of the tent. They built a fire, prepared their pot of coffee, roasted some salted beef, and ate some hard biscuits. It was a rare night with stars and the two sat by the fire with their coffee and enjoyed the sky. The teen shared his experience at the hospital as his young friend started to tell of his first journey when he ran away from home.

As Blake told of his early travels and the reason he left for the war, Matthew asked, "Was your father in the fighting at the Hornets Nest?"

"Thet's whar he was kilt," Blake confirmed.

The Return Home

They never talked about it again. They both knew their connection to one another.

The second day on the road the boys followed the tracks of the Nashville and Chatanooga Railroad southeast in the direction of Tullahoma. The second day ended with a night of sleet. The tent was a comfort, having experienced the same before while on the march, but without any shelter. The sleet ended toward daybreak in a light snowfall. By mid afternoon, the camps around Tullahoma showed in the distance.

"Stop wher ya ar," a voice called from a clump of bushes beside the tracks. A ragged corporal and his likewise ragged companion stepped from behind the bushes.

"We saw ya a quarter mile back," his younger companion pointed out.

"Ain't neve saw a Yank an a Reb travel tagethe afer," the older corporal commented. "Tain't natural. An ya carryin a drum?"

"Are ya really a Reb?" the younger asked.

"Private Bradford James, drummer, with Captain Jonathan Wilson of the 2nd Tennessee," the boy confirmed.

"Who's yer regimental commander?" the other asked.

"I don know. Colonel Butler was killed at Richmond. Colonel Hill had the brigade and General Patrick Cleburne had the division. I last rode courier fer General Wheeler at Perryville. Is Lieutenant Anthony Warren still with the 2nd?"

"Don know. What's wi th sword an who's the Yank?" the older asked again.

"The sword was a friend's and I'm Corporal Matthew Mills under special assignment to get Private James to his home," Matthew replied.

"Does thet mean ya have orders?" The younger asked.

"That's right," the corporal responded, reaching into his coat to pull them out.

The two pickets checked over the orders.

"These are signed by a gen'ral!" the younger exclaimed. "Let's turn 'im ov'r ta the lieutenant."

"Come with us," the older picket instructed.

Matthew and Blake were led to a campfire where several soldiers were gathered and some horses were tied. A rider was sent to find Lieutenant Anthony Warren in the 2nd Tennessee and tell him about the odd pair of strangers found by the pickets. The lieutenant asked that they be brought in.

* * *

Lieutenant Warren folded the paper and handed it back to Matthew. Turning to the rider standing by, he sent him on his way. "Thet'll be all, Private. I'll take it from here."

The picket courier mounted his horse and left.

"Private Bradford James, thought sher ya was dead 'r prisoner. Put yer drum down an stay awhile. Corporal Mills, sher am glad ta meet ya. Thanks fer lookin after ar drummer boy here. Com, find a box an sit by the fire. Coffee's hot." He guided the two to biscuit boxes and handed each a cup.

Blake placed the drum on the ground beside him and the two slid their packs and gear from their backs and settled it on the ground behind them.

"Is Todd here, Lieutenant?" Blake asked as he poured a cup of coffee.

"Sorry, Bradford," Warren replied as he refilled his own cup. "We lost him at Stones River. Nearly half the company is gone. The cap'n 'n Sergeant Taft was kilt. Kramer 'n Fox is in the hospital 'n Kramer might not make it. Private Larken's here." He turned toward the camp. "Private Larken!" he shouted.

To Blake he continued. "Ya stay here tanight. I've sum 'sperience with train transport 'n kin git ya back ta Greeneville."

Aidan Larken arrived and was excited to see Blake.

"Yer 'live!" He rushed to embrace his friend, grateful to see him again. Stepping back for a better look, he asked, "Wher'd ya git the sword?"

"It's a Yank musician's sword. It an this drum b'long'd ta a friend a ar's kilt at Stones River."

"Sit down, Private. Wer gonna hear ther story."

The four talked late into the night, beyond taps and another pot of coffee. Blake and Matthew told of their adventures and the lieutenant and Aidan told what they'd been through. Finally, in the wee hours past midnight the weight of exhaustion took over and the man retired to his tent while the others wrapped themselves in blankets, built up the fire, and settled next to its warmth.

* * *

"Sound reveille, Private." Blake looked up into the warm smile on

Sergeant Harris' face. He held the drum with strap and sticks. "Heerd ya was back. Good ta see ya, James"

"Thanks, Sergeant." Blake stood up and dropped his blanket as he reached for the strap. "I have ma own drum ya know," he said.

"I know, but it's a Yank drum. This ne's yers from afer." Harris smiled.

Snapping the drum in place, the boy took the sticks and tapped out reveille. The new day was official.

"Bradford," Lieutenant Warren began, "would ya two stay with us taday? I'll 'range fer tickets ta Greeneville and fer food 'long the way. We don't do much now days but camp chores 'n culd sher use yer comp'ny."

"We could use the rest, Sir," Matthew replied. "How about it, Bradford?"

"Yes, Sir." It was agreed.

The day drifted by lazily as the boys visited with the few members of the company who were left. During the early afternoon, they took their guns and went on a hunting expedition with Aidan. The three even brought a wild turkey back for the stew pot. Foraging in a corn field along the way added a little more than a dozen broken ears of corn. True, the coons had gotten to them first, but there were still a few kernels left on each ear.

General Cleburne had heard of the visitors by way of a picket report and stopped by with his staff in tow, in need of some good news. He was introduced to the boys and stepped down from his horse to greet them.

"Kin I see yer orders, Corporal," he asked. After reading them carefully, he handed them to a staff officer. "Captain, kin ya add a line, "to any who meet these boys in the execution of this order, you are instructed to assist them in any way, by order of Patrick Cleburne, Maj. Gen., 2nd Div., Army of Tennessee." He took the paper from the captain, signed it, and returned it to Matthew.

The teen came to attention and saluted with a, "Thank you, General." General Cleburne nodded in acknowledgement.

"I am grateful fer sumthin good in this horrid affair an wish ya both God speed on a safe journey. I'm pleased ta hav met ya. Take care a them, Lieutenant."

"Yes, Sir," Warren saluted. It was returned as the general remounted his horse.

"Gentlemen." He nodded one last time, then spurred his horse onward.

Ecstatic smiles creased dirt-encrusted faces all around.

"I don't b'lieve it." Blake could hardly talk in his excitement.

"You boys ar som'thin special." The lieutenant, too, could hardly speak.

Too soon the reunion ended as the day drifted into night and the gathering of friends cleaned up after a dinner of roasted turkey and corn remains, along with some hard bread and coffee.

After breakfast of bacon and bread, Lieutenant Anthony Warren along with Private Aidan Larken escorted their friends to the train station at Tullahoma. Blake and Matthew kept their packs and weapons, sword and drum with them as they struggled up the steps into the front coach of the train. The lieutenant had given Matthew the packet of tickets, instructions, and army meal vouchers for food along the railroad part of the journey. The boys settled in a pair of facing seats bedside the window to wave goodbye to their friends as the train pulled out. The sword, drum and packs were stowed on the empty facing seat.

Warren and Larken stood by the track and watched as the train headed south. After the distant smoke of the engine faded into the morning mists, they turned to walk back to the camp.

* * *

The journey had its moments of danger. At various stops along the way there were soldiers who got on the train and others who got off. More than once the boys caught an uncomfortable glance from passenger or soldier. But the conductor had read the orders and interrupted any who might threaten the two. To be safe, they remained in their seats until they had to get off at Stevenson to change onto the railroad north that would connect to the Virginia and Tennessee Railroad around Chattanooga.

As Matthew and Blake descended the coach steps to the station platform, a group of hardened soldiers surrounded them.

"Ya two is goin wi' us," a corporal ordered.

The conductor watched helplessly and called to the station master. "Harvey! Git ther captain! Those boys have orders 'n ther in trouble!"

The stationmaster quickly ducked back into the station and reemerged with an officer. He pointed toward the group of soldiers who were dragging the boys off and passed the conductor's message to him.

"Hold on, men!" the captain called. But they ignored him. "Ya'r ordered ta stop!" he shouted. They continued on. The officer drew his

The Return Home

revolver and fired into the air. The group stopped. He holstered his gun.

They turned to face the officer. "Yer not stoppin us from ar bounty money!" the corporal shouted back.

"Ya wait where ya ar!" He approached the group. "Let go those boys an stan back!"

The captain faced Matthew. "Ya have orders, Corporal?"

"Yes, Sir." He reached into his coat and pulled out the papers. Sorting out the orders, he handed them to the captain.

As the officer read the orders, his face registered surprise, then anger as he addressed the soldiers before him. "Do ya boys want ta go b'fer a court martial?" He held up the paper. "These boys have orders a safe passage from Brigadeer General Cruft…"

"Don't mean nothin," the corporal interrupted. "He's a Yank general."

"And," the captain continued, "they's also signed by Major General Cleburne of the Army of Tennessee."

There was a stunned silence.

"The gen'ral writes," he read from the orders, "you are instructed to assist them in any way." He handed the paper back to Matthew who returned it to his coat with the other papers.

"Wer awf'l sorry, Sir. We didn't know." The corporal stood awkwardly, not sure of what to expect. "My 'pology, Boys. What kin we do?"

"Thank ya, Cap'n," Blake whispered, still frightened from the experience.

"We need to get on the train through Knoxville that goes to Greeneville," Matthew added.

"Corporal," the captain addressed the Confederates, "Why don ya all stay wi' these boys an keep em safe ta git on ther train."

"Yes, Sir. We will, Sir. Okay, Boys?" He saluted the captain.

"Thank ya." The captain returned the salute then turned back to the station.

Suddenly the boys were famous and the soldiers couldn't be more friendly. As they waited for the northbound train the boys and their escort sat among the cases of freight and exchanged stories about their war experiences. Blake put the drum on its side on the wooden decking and sat on it while Matthew found a comfortable crate. Blake explained how he had been with the 2nd Tennessee, fallen at Perryville, and ended up with the 31st Illinois, rescued by Matthew. They both told of Stones River. Their escorts told of the war they had seen. All agreed they would be happy for it to end so they could all go home.

Interrupted by an approaching whistle, the boys were accompanied to the train and on their way once more.

At Chatanooga, the orders were again needed to transfer trains around the city and make final connection to the Virginia and Tennessee Railroad. At Greeneville, remembering the problems Jackson and James had encountered, Blake decided they should check in with the stationmaster. They were glad they did. He informed them that bounty hunters were active in the area, after any bounty they could get, legitimate or otherwise. The stationmaster suggested that they use their vouchers to stay over at the hotel and await the next freight wagons from Shelby. There were deliveries for the return trip and they could ride back with the wagons.

So it was that on Wednesday, the 18th of February, Blake and Matthew found themselves on a wagon leaving Greeneville toward Shelby, finally relieved of their gear and sword and drum as they were place in the bed of the wagon for the trip.

* * *

Five days later, the wagons arrived at Shelby. Filthy from weeks of travel, the exhausted boys climbed down from the wagon as it pulled up in the yard behind the Bradford General Store and Freight business. They boys reached their packs and gear from the wagon and put it over their shoulders and on their backs. Blake slung the drum and sword belt on his shoulder as they walked toward the building.

"I cain't wait ta git home!" Blake exclaimed as they walked around the building to the front door.

"Bradford?" Matthew asked. "Why is your name on this business?" He stood staring at the sign above the front porch.

"This is ma uncle's business. I'm not Bradford James. I made up the name when I fust met the lieutenant." They started toward the steps. "My name is Blake Bradford. James is our field hand's son."

The two climbed the front steps to the front porch and entered.

"Blake!" Justin shouted as they entered the store. He ran around from behind the counter to take the boy by the shoulders and look him over. "Ya look like Hell! And you stink somethin' fierce! Ya okay? An what's wi the drum an sword?"

"I'm fine, Justin. But a bath would sur feel great. They was a friend's who was killed in the war." He turned to Matthew. "This here's Corporal Matthew Mills, ma friend."

"What's wi' the blue uniform?" He reached out to shake the teen's hand.

"He was in the Union army," Blake explained.

"Was?" Matthew asked.

"Yer orders is done. I'm home."

"Not quite." Justin cut in. "But I'll git us horses from Homer an we'll be there real soon."

Word rapidly spread around Shelby as the three walked over to Homer's livery barn and borrowed and saddled three horses. The Bradford boy was home, and he was alive!

The three riders raced south on the road to the Bradford Plantation, packs and guns bouncing wildly on their backs, the drum clipped to its strap with the sword belted around his waist and bouncing at Blake's side. It was Monday late morning, the yard was empty as the hands were off in the fields. A snow-covered landscape didn't mean no work. Sammy was at the pump getting water for his ma as she was busy in the kitchen fixing dinner.

The boy looked up, startled by the sound of galloping horses, then ran to the back door.

"Ma, riders comin!" he shouted.

Sarah rushed out to the back porch, followed closely by Celia, and the Bradford children and their mother.

"They's two soldiers," Raymond observed.

"One's Fed'ral an one's Confed'rate," Celia added.

"They's wi' Justin," Charlotte said. "I wonda what they's wantin."

Ruth Ann noticed first. "It's Blake!" she screamed.

"Oh my God!" Charlotte cried, tears bursting forth uncontrollably. "Blake, yer alive!" She dashed down the steps, racing to the boy in grey as he pulled up his horse, dropped to the ground, slipped off his pack, drum, and rifle, and jumped into his mother's arms, sword dangling at his side.

Quickly all gathered around the boy and his mother, locked in a tear-filled embrace, holding each other, locked together in a brief eternity.

Suddenly, Matthew was overcome in his own deep grief as he felt alone and so very guilty for the death of his friend's father. Sitting in the saddle and shaken by his own wrenching sobs, he leaned forward and buried his face in the mane of the horse. There he cried his heart out.

While all attention was on the boy and his mother, Justin noticed the misery of the older boy. He guided his horse to Matthew's side.

"What's wrong, Matthew?"

Without moving he mumbled between sobs, "It hurts so. I hate this war." He could manage no more.

The man rested a consoling hand on the boy's back and sat with him. Sarah walked over, then looked up to Justin with a silent question of concern.

"He is sufferin sumthin terrible," the man answered. "I've no idea why, but it's very deep inside a him."

The woman reached up to help Matthew down from the horse. He let her guide him to the ground, then buried his face on her shoulder and shook with silent sobbing. She embraced him, rubbing his back gently, and whispered, "It's gonna be all right. Yer home now."

Finally, between fits of tears, Charlotte looked up. "Sammy, run an tell Marse Daniel thet Blake is home! Hurry!"

The boy was off as fast as his feet could carry him.

* * *

The horses were tied in the stable. The field hands were given the rest of the day off. The family was gathered around the dining room table. The sword, drum, packs, and gear had been left in the hall at the foot of the stairs.

Justin, who had been invited to stay over until the afternoon, turned to Matthew, who was sitting beside him.

"Kin I see yer orders," he asked.

The youth took his papers from inside his coat, sorted out the orders, and handed them to the man. He opened them and read them carefully. Conversation at the table quieted as others looked on. After a few minutes of quiet, Justin looked up,

"This is Private Matthew Mills. These orders promote him ta corporal an detach him from the army ta bring Blake home. Upon completion of this assignment, he is discharged from the army for medical reasons suffered from the war." He began to loose his voice as he finally whispered, "An ther signed by gen'rals from both armies."

There was stunned silence from those gathered at the table and from the servants standing to the side. Some wept silently, overcome by the emotion felt toward the older boy.

"May I see thet, Justin?" Daniel asked.

The paper was passed around the table to the uncle. He looked it over carefully, then paused. An idea formed, but he held on to it momentarily.

"Blake." He reached the paper toward his nephew. "Take this into the parlor and put it in the front of the family Bible."

The boy stood to do as he was told. Then the man turned toward Matthew.

"Son, if you have no home to go back to, then let this become your home."

Blake froze in the doorway and turned to the conversation.

"But I…"

"Yes!" Blake interrupted. "Say yes!"

"But I…"

"It's okay!" Tears welled up in the boy's eyes. "Jest say yes!"

Matthew looked directly into his young friend's eyes and whispered, "Yes."

They smiled at each other as Blake turned back to do as he had been told.

When he returned to his seat, his uncle asked, "Do ya know what tamorra is?"

Settling into his chair he responded, "I"ve long ago lost knowin what one day is into anotha."

"Da ya know what month this is?"

"No."

"Tamorra's yer birthday. Ya'll be twelve."

Silence.

"You'll be old enough to be a drummer boy," Matthew stated.

"Oh."

Laughter rippled around the room.

"Justin," Daniel turned to his store manager. "When ya git back, close the business fer tamorra and tell ever'on as we're havin a celebration tamorra, bring ther fam'lies. I'll tell Jackson ta send James ta the Parker Plantation an tell Tyler thet Blake is home an ta git ov'r here as quick as he kin. Sarah, take charge a the house. Jackson 'll take care a settin up outside. Justin, go right back an send out the big tents from the army's order. They'll git em used."

All was put into motion for the preparation for a grand celebration of Blake's birthday and his safe return.

"Kin I ware ma uniform?" Blake asked. "An Matthew, too?"

"Yes," Charlotte responded before anyone could say otherwise. "I'm proud of you both. Celia," she called to the kitchen. "See ta the house staff ta gittin baths fer these boys an gittin ther uniforms cleaned up."

"Yes, M'am," came the reply from the doorway.

Then Blake's mother rose from the table and walked to the library. All eyes followed her out of the room, wondering why she had left. In a moment, she returned with something carried folded into the front of her dress. She approached her son.

"Son, I want ya ta wear this with yer uniform."

She opened the dress to reveal his father's revolver. Reverently the boy lifted the holstered gun from his mother's dress and held it in his arms. Tears streamed down his face as he looked into his mother's eyes with a sense of pride, and nodded his approval.

* * *

Blake showed Matthew where to put his musket and cartridges in the library, then had him bring his pack and gear upstairs to the bedroom. Blake brought the drum and sword up with his pack and gear and placed the drum on its side beside the wardrobe where he could see it always. The sword was carefully hung inside the wardrobe. The packs would be cared for later. By evening, the family and their guest were gathered in the parlor. The boys were cleaned up and refreshed. Blake had outgrown his clothes and there were none for Matthew, so Blake's mother had taken them into the attic and found a trunk of his father's clothes from when he was a boy. It was an emotional search, but they found things to fit each boy.

During the evening's conversation, Blake finally learned what had happened when he left.

"When ya didn't cum back," his mother explained. "Yer uncle went ta Shelby to find ya. Prince was at the livery, but there was no sign a ya afta leavin 'im thar."

"Jackson said as they'd warned ya of abolitionists," Daniel added. "We fig'red they took ya, an sent search parties through the country. But afta weeks a lookin, we fig'red they'd kilt ya fer spite."

"Even though Tyler said as ya'd talked 'bout it, I neva fig'red ya'd gone ta the war." His mother leaned forward in her chair. "I sher does thank ya Matthew fer gittin him home safe."

"Yes, M'am," the boy managed. It was going to be hard not explaining.

The family retired for the night. Matthew would stay in Blake's room until they were ready to separate so he could have a room of his own. They changed into night shirts, a luxury they had forgotten ever existed. Crawling into Blake's bed, they lay silent for several minutes. Then Matthew observed, "It's like it never happened. It's like we're here in this life and our life in the war was just a bad dream."

"But we know it wern't," Blake glanced at his friend. "We know it's real an as we got friends who is still there."

"Uh huh."

They lay there without saying any more for several minutes.

"Night. Ain't nothin like bein back in ma own bed."

Nothing more was said. Each was lost in his own thoughts until finally drifting off to sleep.

* * *

Tuesday was the 24th of February. Blake could hardly believe it was his birthday. The uniforms had been brushed as clean as the wool would allow, tears had been repaired, and loose buttons resecured. The plantation was alive with preparations for a grand celebration, in spite of the snow on the ground. Large army hospital tents had been delivered from the freight yard and were being set up by the field hands. Once up, the snow would be cleared from the grounds inside and tables and benches would be set up.

In the early hours of the morning, Blake and Matthew had emptied their packs and put the contents away. The drum strap and sticks were set aside, then brought down to the center hall and placed with Christopher's drum at the bottom of the stairs,

The boys had gone to the front porch to watch for Tyler's carriage. There was a chill in the air, but relief in that there was no snow or sleet or rain. Sitting in the rocking chairs, Blake told Matthew of the battle that had taken place back in the summer. It was hard to realize that it really wasn't that long ago. He had only been away to the war for a little more than six months.

The rattle of harness chains drew their attention to the road and a carriage coming up from the south. They watched as Tyler approached, traveling up the pike, and turning into the lane. Bristol brought the team around expertly to the front steps. Blake descended the steps to greet his friend. Having the benefit of months of experience, Tyler quickly maneuvered out of the carriage to balance himself on his crutches, held by Bristol until he took them. Matthew stood aside as the two worked their way up the steps.

Finally on the porch, Tyler was introduced to Matthew. He could not bring himself to accept the offered hand. Shock clouded his face. "Blake, he killed your pa!"

"I know. He knows I know. We've both known these past weeks. He was a soldier and did as he had ta. Now he's like a brother ta me. I've fergiven him."

Back Album

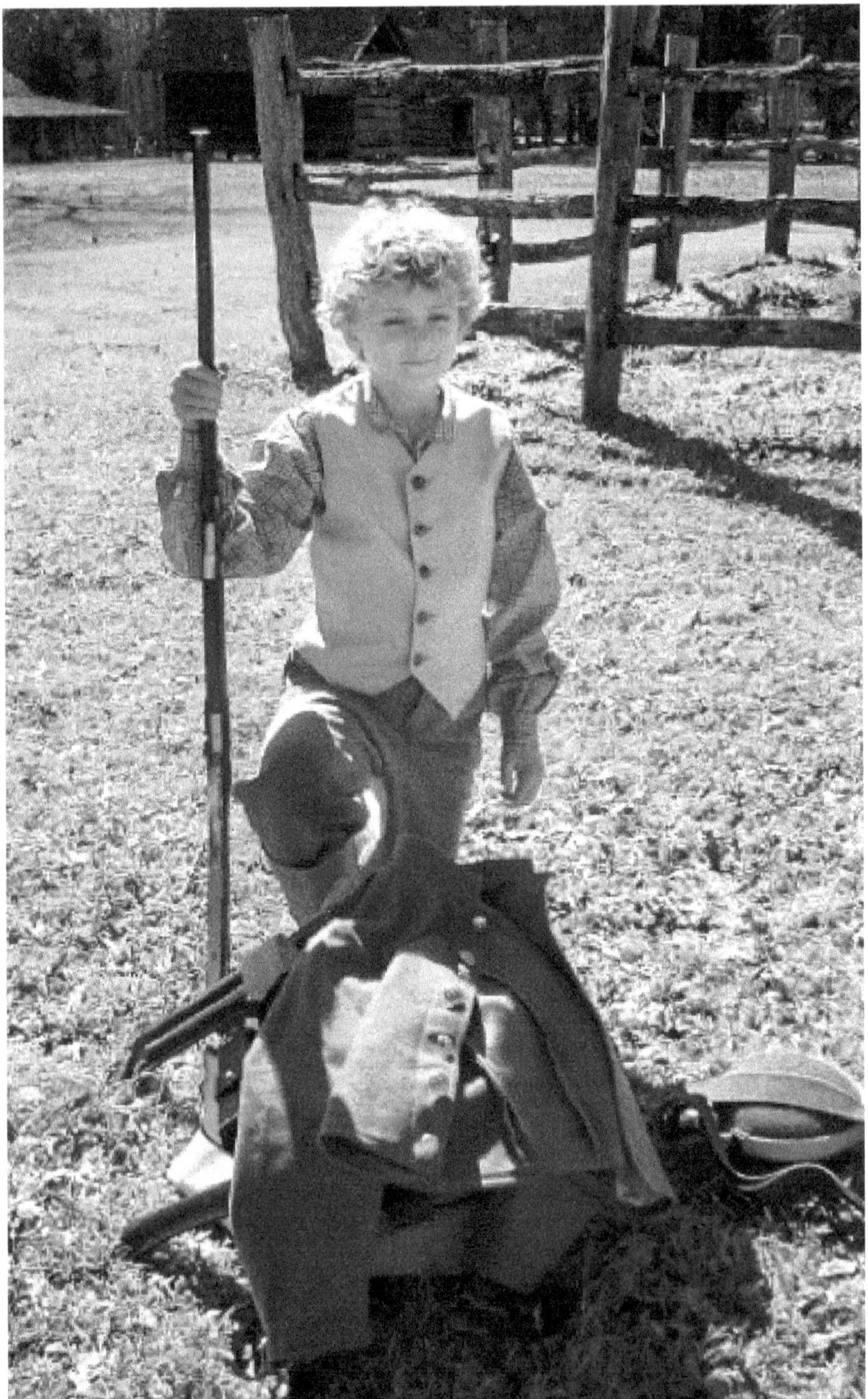

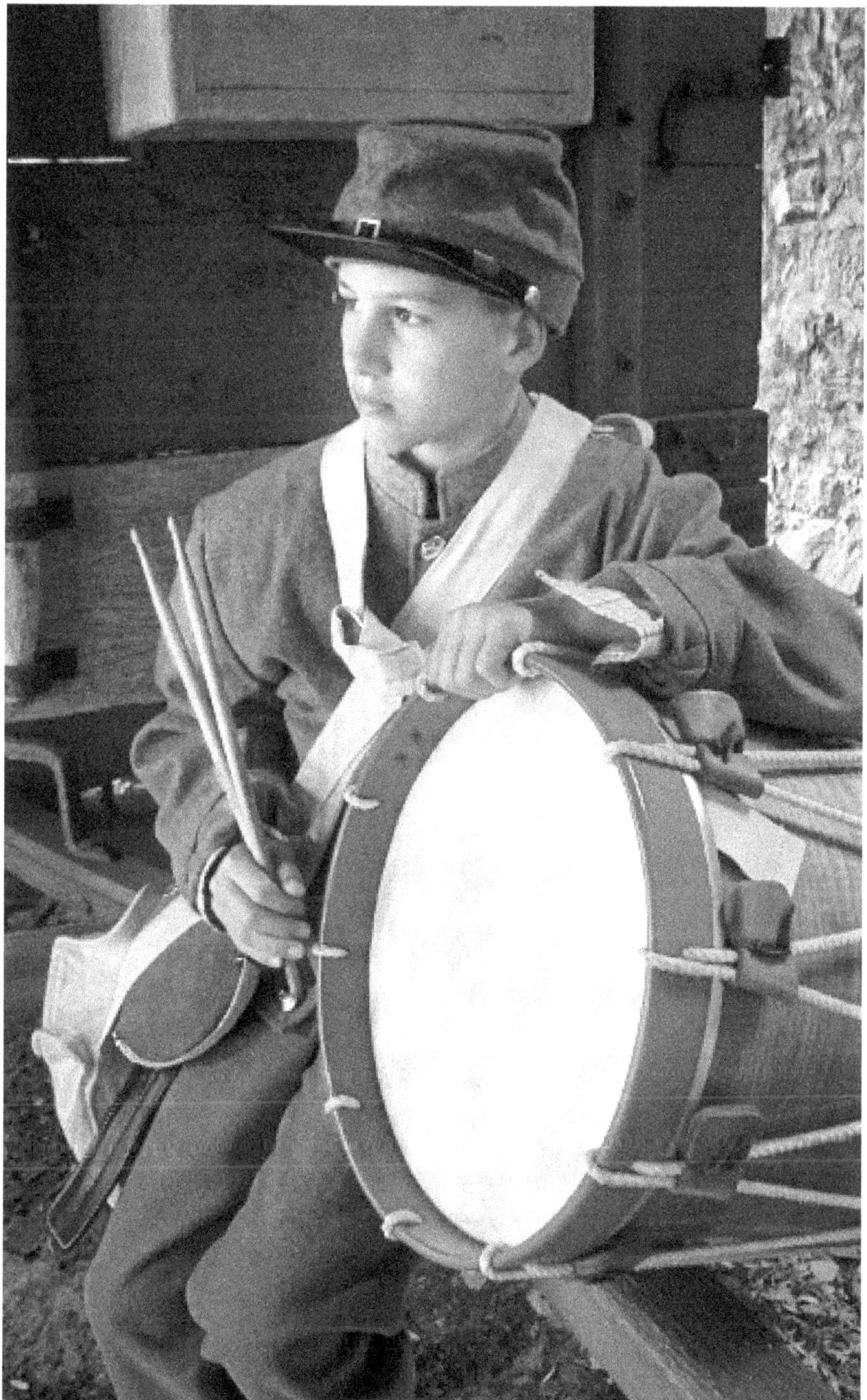

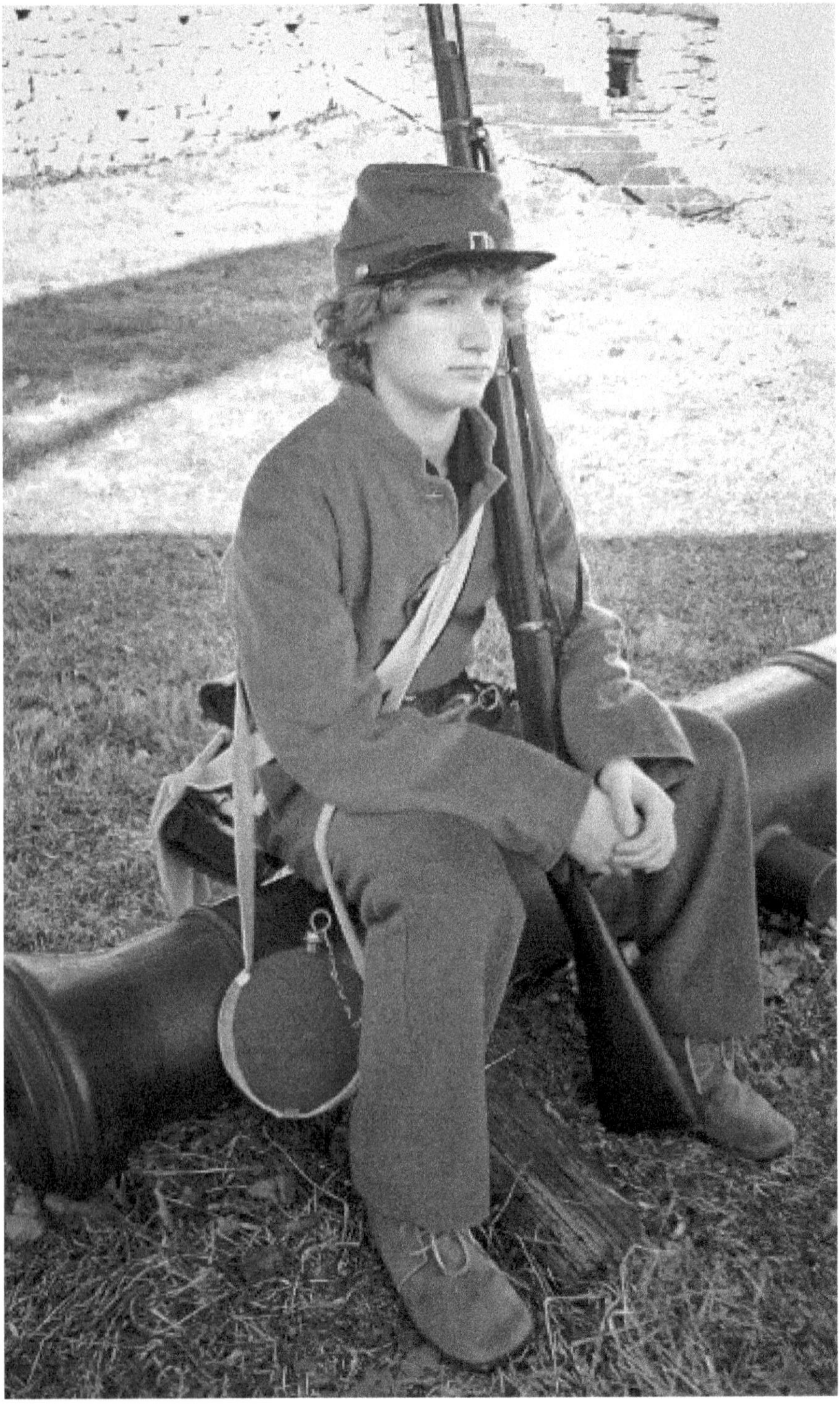

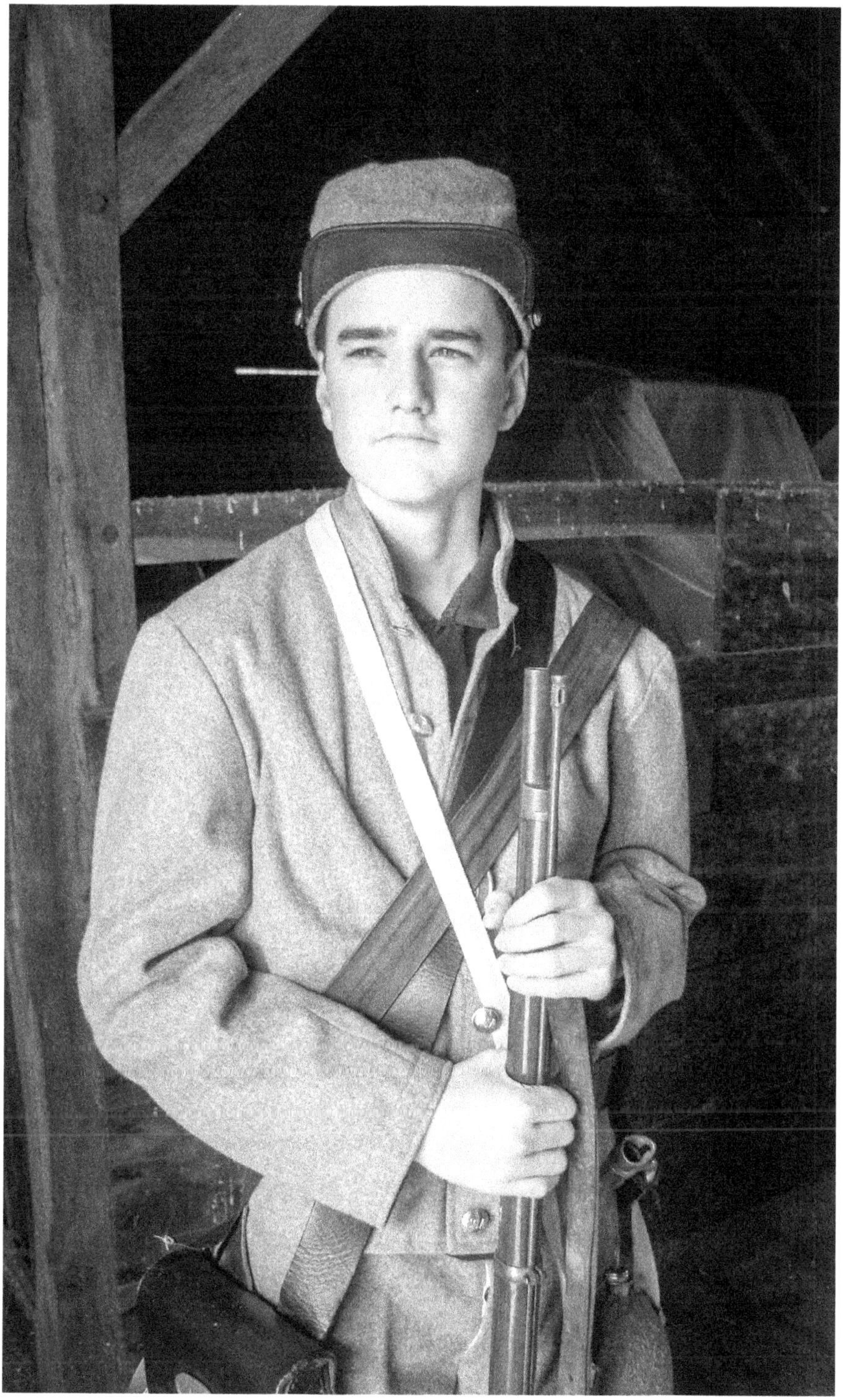

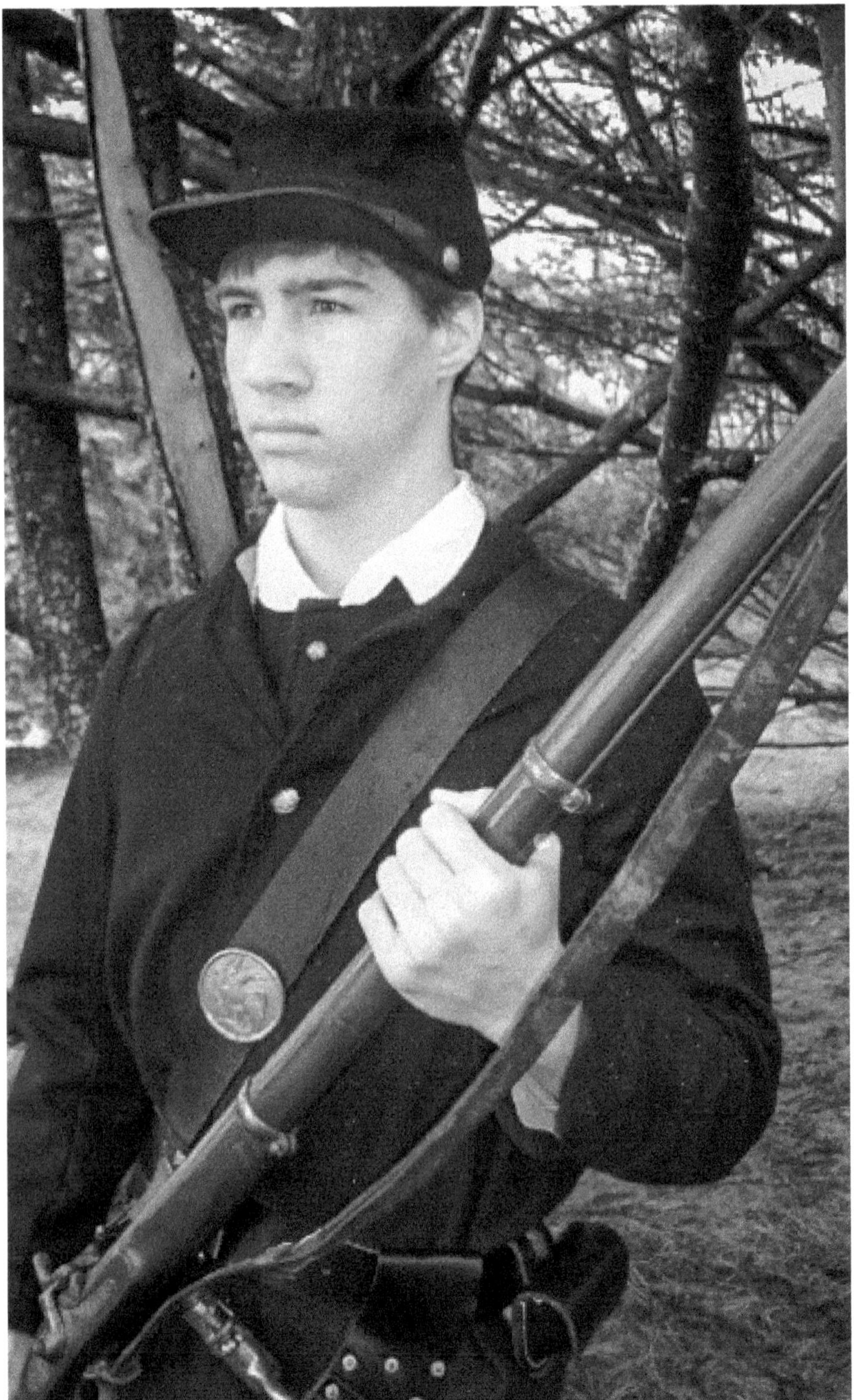

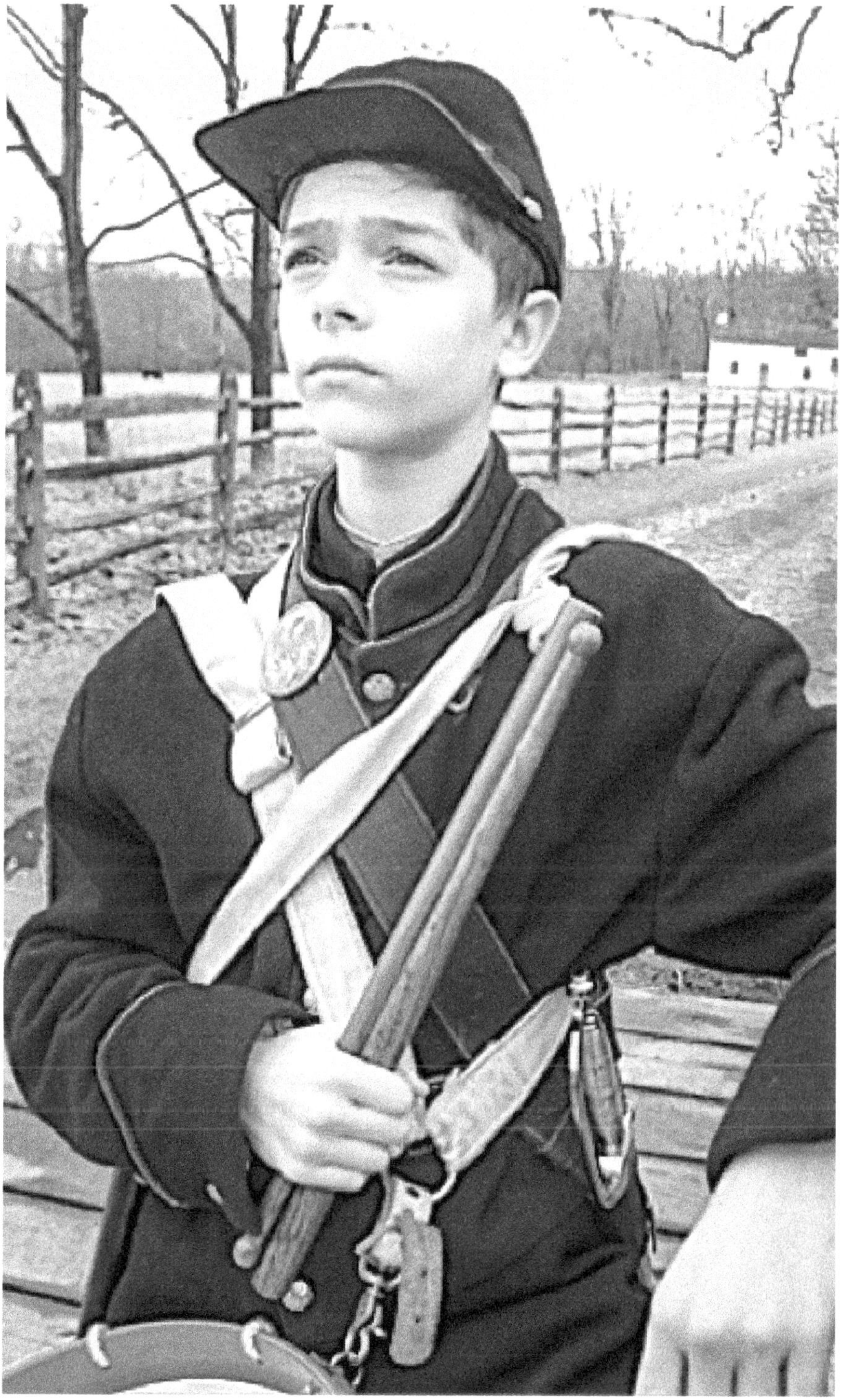

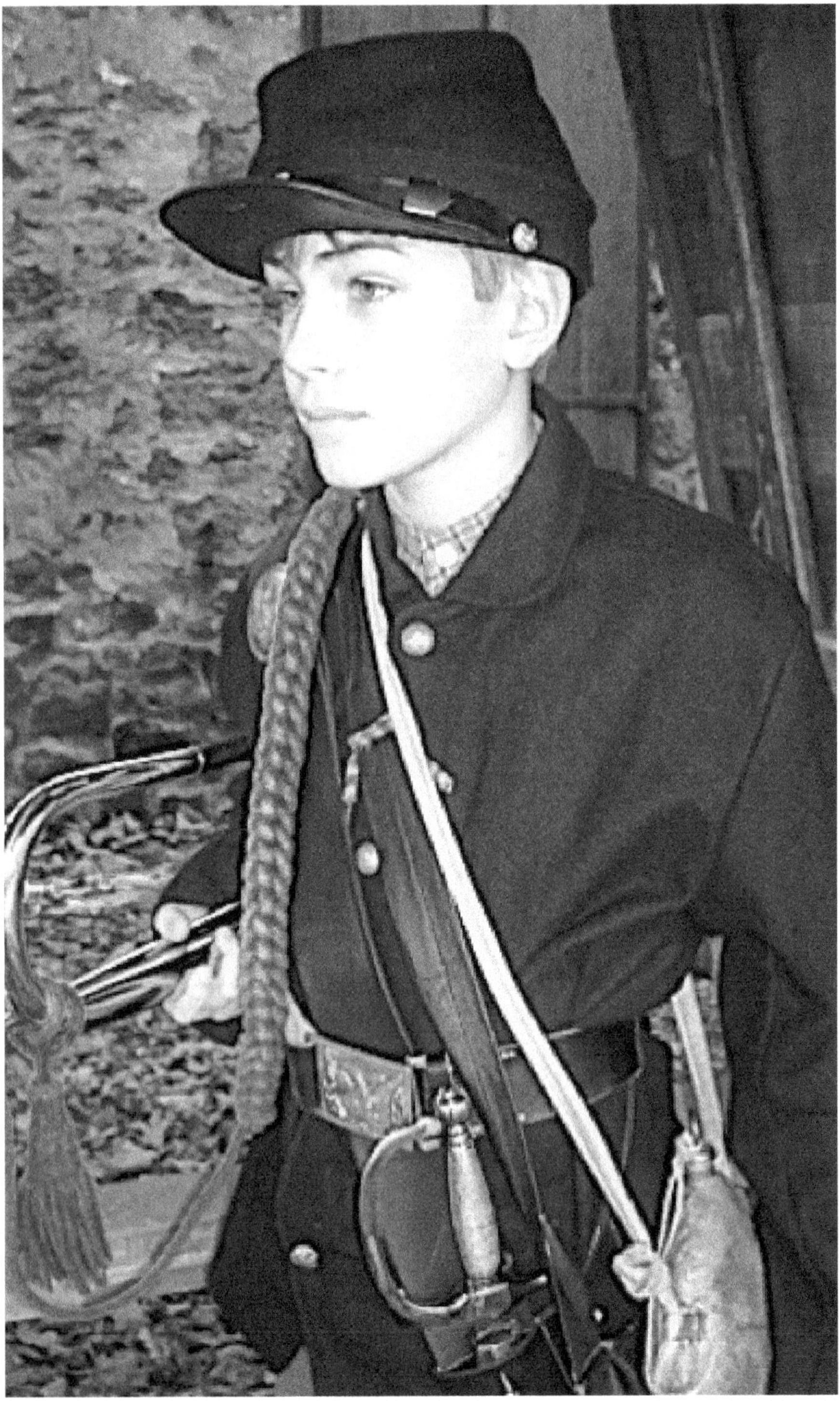

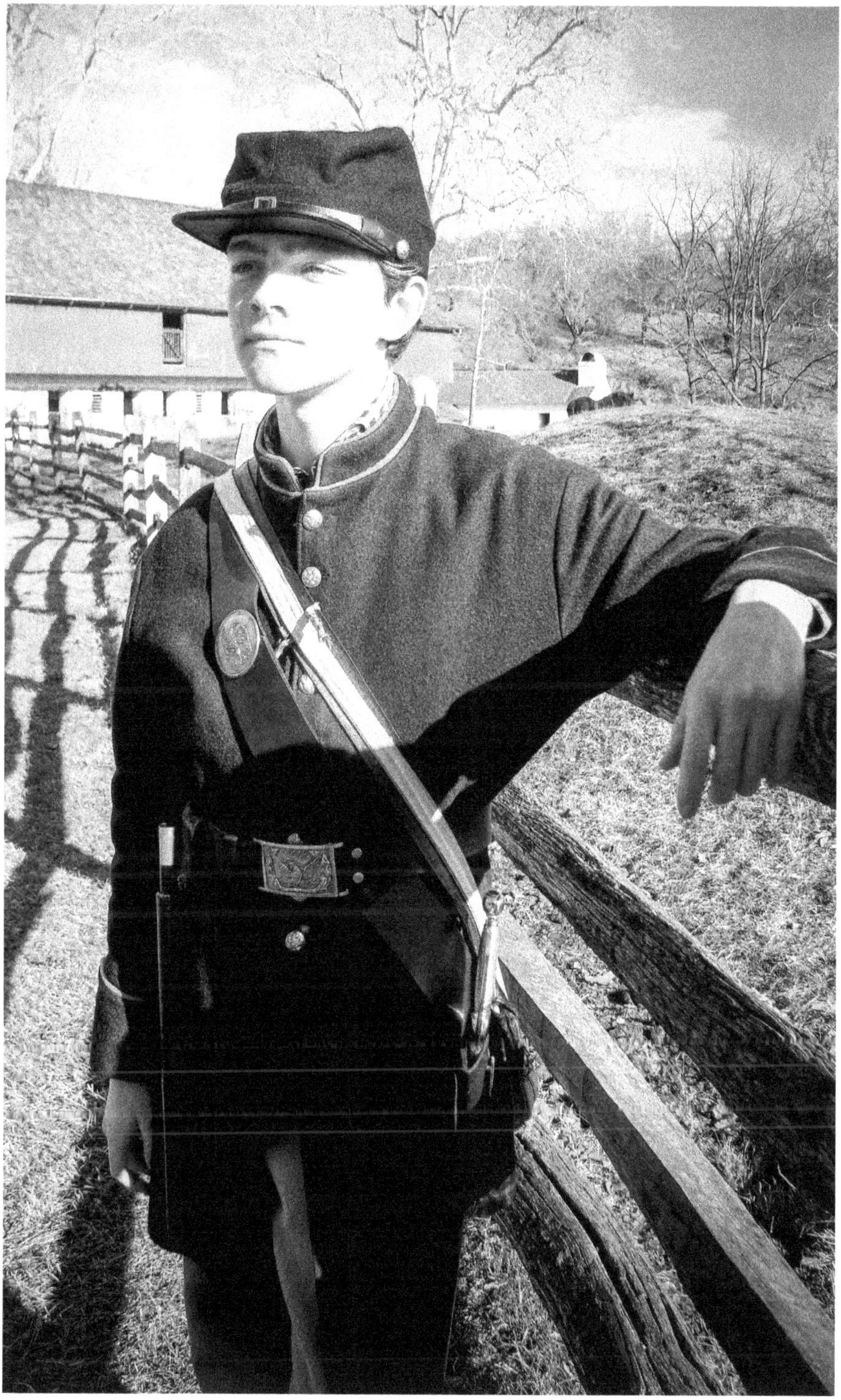

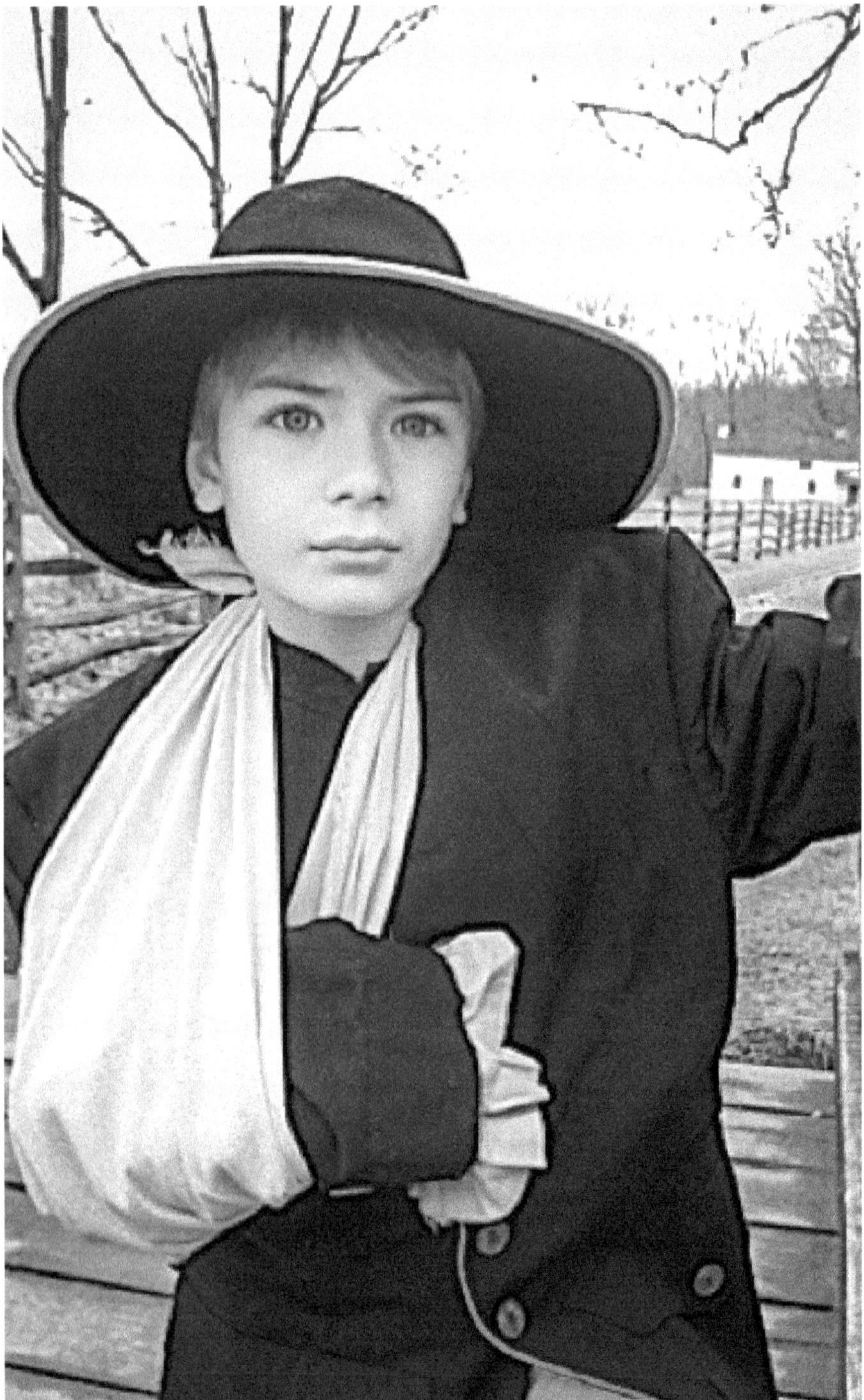

References

The Kentucky Campaign 1862

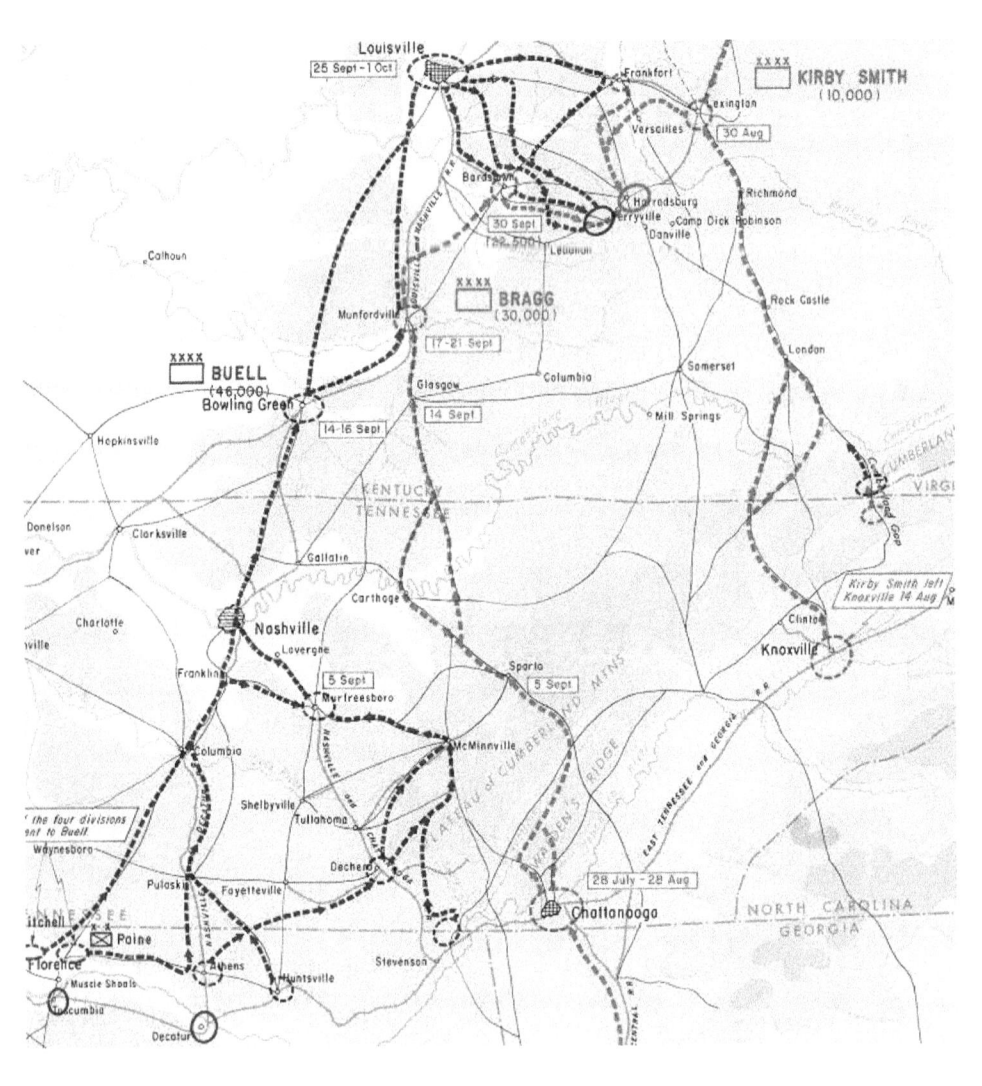

source:
http://americancivilwar.com/campaigns/Confederate_Heartland_Campaign.html
[americancivilwar.com/all articles are public domain]

Army of Northern Virginia or Army of the Patomac or etc.

[commanded by a general]
3-6 army corps

Corp
[commanded by a lieutenant-general]
average of 3 divisions plus a unit of artillery

Division
[commanded by a major-general]
about 5 brigades plus a battalion [5 batteries] of artillery
note:- a battery of artillery included about 6 cannons with caissons of ammunition, limbers for each, horses, men, and officers

Brigade
[commanded by a brigadeer-general]
about 5 regiments

Regiment
[commanded by a colonel]
up to 10 companies

Company
[commanded by a captain]
2-4 platoons, about 50 men plus officers

Platoon
[commanded by a lieutenant]
about 12-20 men and officers

note: When armies were at full strength, companies tended to have 100 soldiers and officers, later in the war some might be down to less than 36.

The History Behind Blake's Story

In Blake's Story, historic events bring two boys together, one of whom has killed the father of the other. In order for this to happen, the regiments in the story have to be in the right place at the right time. Here are the regiments and here are their relevant histories.

Micah Bradford raised a company to support a friend of his in Tennessee. His company became part of the 19th Tennessee infantry regiment under Colonel David H. Cummings which, by the time of Shiloh, was within the Third Brigade under Colonel Winfield S. Stratham in the Reserve Corps of the Confederate Army under Brigadeer General John C. Breckinridge.

Matthew Mills was a private in the 31st Indiana under Colonel Charles Cruft and, at Shiloh, in the Third Brigade under Brigadeer General Jacob G. Lauman within the Fourth Division of the Union Army under Brigadeer General Stephen A. Hurlbut.

This is the map of events between four and five on the afternoon of April 7, 1862.

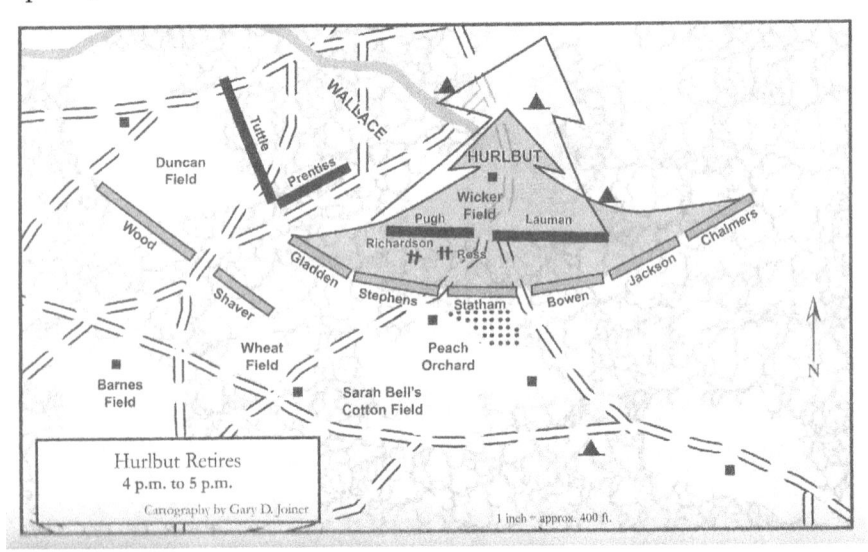

Cunningham, O. Edward, *Shiloh and the Western Campaign of 1862* (Savas Beatie, New York. 2007), page 274

Note the location of Statham's Regiment and Lauman's regiment. The 19th was "on the right" [Cunningham, O. Edward, *Shiloh and the Western Campaign of 1862* (Savas Beatie, New York. 2007), page 272]. Presumably, the 31st Indiana was on the right being listed first in the order of battle. This would put Micah and Matthew opposite each other at this point in the battle enabling Matthew to kill Blake's father at this point.

412 *Shiloh and the Western Campaign of 1862*   Appendix 1: Confederate Order of Battle   405

Fourth Division
Brig. Gen. Stephen A. Hurlbut

First Brigade
Col. Nelson G. Williams (wounded), 3d Iowa
Col. Isaac C. Pugh, 41st Illinois
28th Illinois:
Col. Amory K. Johnson
32d Illinois:
Col. John Logan (wounded)
41st Illinois:
Col. Isaac C. Pugh
Lieut. Col. Ansel Tupper (killed)
Maj. John Warner
Capt. John H. Nale
3d Iowa:
Maj. William M. Stone (captured)
Lieut. George W. Crosley

Second Brigade
Col. James C. Veatch, 25th Indiana
14th Illinois:
Col. Cyrus Hall
15th Illinois:
Lieut. Col. Edward F. W. Ellis (killed)
Capt. Louis D. Kelley
Lieut. Col. William Cam, 14th Illinois
46th Illinois:
Col. John A. Davis (wounded)
Lieut. Col. John J. Jones
25th Indiana:
Lieut. Col. William H. Morgan (wounded)
Maj. John W. Foster

Third Brigade
Brig. Gen. Jacob G. Lauman
31st Indiana:
Col. Charles Cruft (wounded)
Lieut. Col. John Osborn
44th Indiana:
Col. Hugh B. Reed

Second Brigade
Brig. Gen. John S. Bowen (wounded)
Col. John D. Martin
9th Arkansas:
Col. Isaac L. Dunlop
10th Arkansas:
Col. Thomas H. Merrick
2d Confederate:
Col. John D. Martin
Maj. Thomas H. Mangum
1st Missouri:
Col. Lucius L. Rich
Pettus Flying Artillery or Hudson's Mississippi Battery:
Capt. Alfred Hudson
Watson's Louisiana Battery
Capt. Allen A. Burlsey
Thompson's Company, Kentucky Cavalry:
Capt. Phil. B. Thompson

Third Brigade
Col. Winfield S. Statham, 15th Mississippi
15th Mississippi:
Maj. William F. Brantley (wounded)
Capt. Lamkin S. Terry
22d Mississippi:
Col. Frank Schaller (wounded)
Lieut. Col. Charles S. Nelms (mortally wounded)
Maj. James S. Prestidge
19th Tennessee:
Col. David H. Cummings (wounded)
Lieut. Col. Francis M. Walker
20th Tennessee:
Col. Joel A. Battle (wounded and captured)
Maj. Patrick Duffy
28th Tennessee:
Col. John P. Murray
45th Tennessee:
Lieut. Col. Ephraim F. Lytle
Rutledge's Tennessee Battery:
Capt. Arthur M. Rutledge

Cunningham, O. Edward, *Shiloh and the Western Campaign of 1862* (Savas Beatie, New York. 2007), pages 412/405

Note that the letter informing the family of Micah's death is from Colonel Cummings.

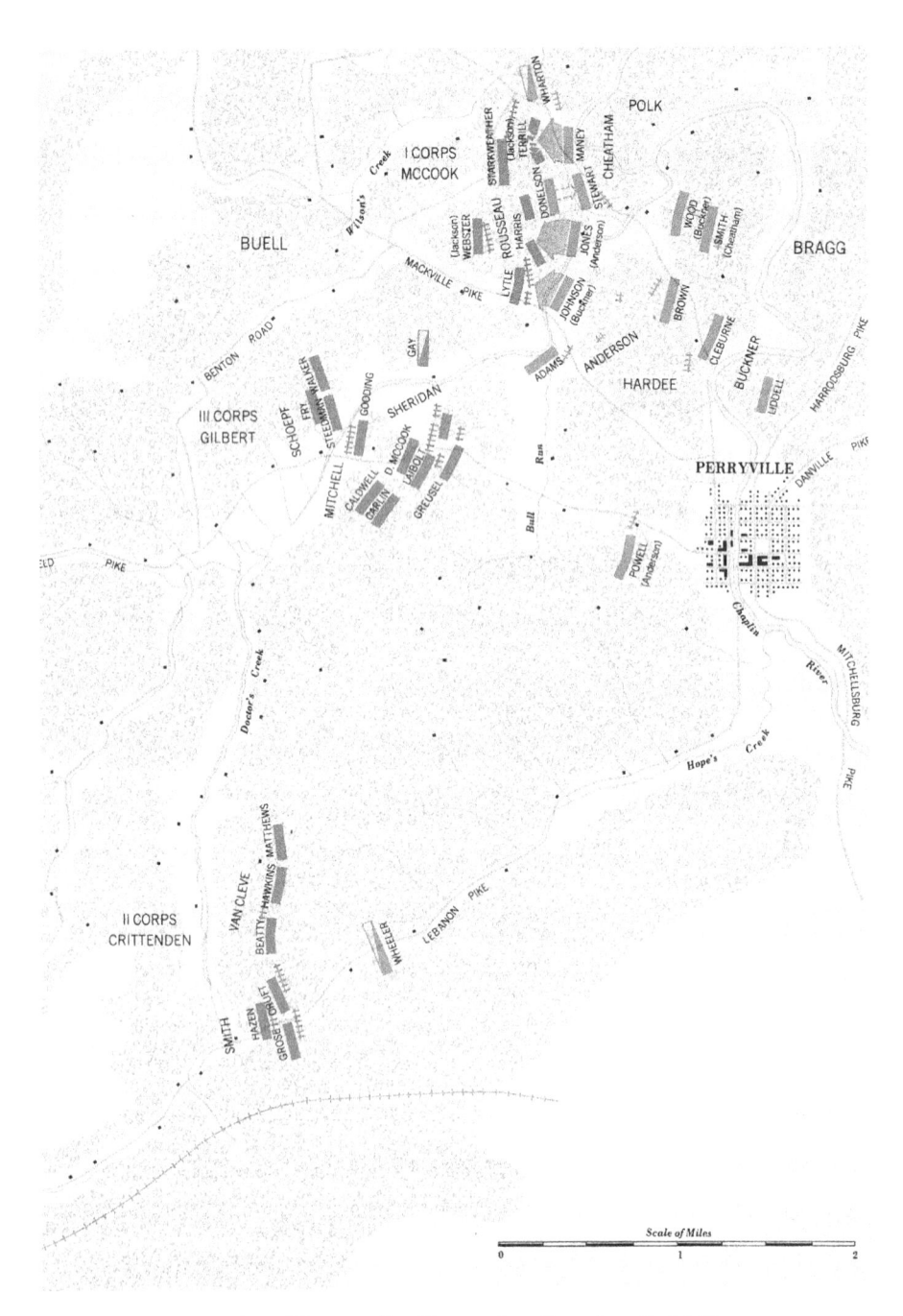

Battle of Perryville, Kentucky, October 8, 1862
Street, James, Jr. and Time-Life editors, *The Struggle for Tennessee, Tupelo to Stones River*, (Time-Life Books, Alexandria, Virginia, 1985), 63

This sets the stage for the evolution of the second coming together of units so that Blake ends up in the same regiment as Matthew. When Blake runs away to the war, he ends up with the small company from the 2nd Tennessee Volunteer Infantry regiment, detached from General Benjamin J. Hill's brigade of General Patrick R. Cleburne's Division of General Kirby Smith's army, as he hides in a wagon between Shelby and Greeneville. The supply company rejoins the army, operating in southeastern Kentucky and Blake finds himself replacing the drummer boy who has taken ill. For lack of a drum Blake rides courier for the regiment's Colonel John A. Butler into battle at Richmond, Kentucky.

Over the weeks that followed, Cleburne's division was returned to General Braxton Bragg's army as the two Confederate armies advanced toward Perryville, Kentucky. However, in the battle to come, the 31st Indiana of which Matthew was a soldier, would not be near the main battle. The 31st, under Charles Cruft was with General Thomas T. Crittenden and the II Corps on the Lebanon Pike, southwest of Perryville. The primary Confederate force on the Lebanon Pike was General Joseph Wheeler's cavalry. As the 2nd Tennessee set camp with Bragg's army, north of Perryville, events play out that see Blake assigned to Wheeler's staff as a courier. The events involving Major General William Hardee and General Joseph Wheeler and their meeting before the battle, did take place. The history is real. When the battle began to unfold, Blake was with Wheeler and Matthew was with Cruft, under the overall command of General Crittenden.

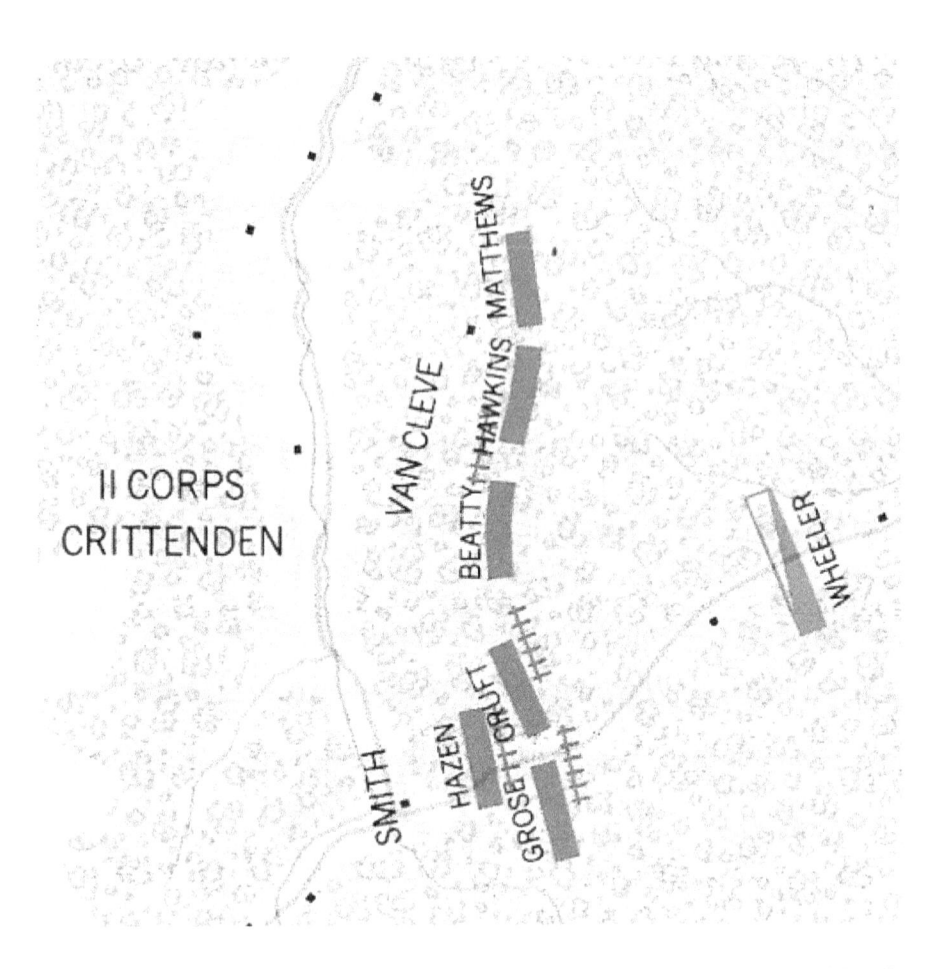

Street, James, Jr. and Time-Life editors, *The Struggle for Tennessee, Tupelo to Stones River*, (Time-Life Books, Alexandria, Virginia, 1985), 63, outtake

Thus, as the story unfolds during the events of the battle at Perryville that play out on the Lebanon Pike, Blake falls wounded and is taken in by Matthew and John, thus saving him from possible death and putting the two boys together to allow the balance of the story to play out.

Two historic events were critical to the historic accuracy of Blake's Story. First, Matthew and Micah had to be at the same place at the same time during the battle at Shiloh for Matthew to kill Blake's father. Second, Matthew and Blake had to be at the same place at the same time during the battle at Perryville for Blake to end up in the same unit with Matthew. This is the history that enables ***Blake's Story, Revenge and Forgiveness,*** to unfold with historic truth.

The rest of the history behind these regiments and their portrayal within Blake's Story, can be found by reading the references gathered in the sources in the reference section in the back of the book.

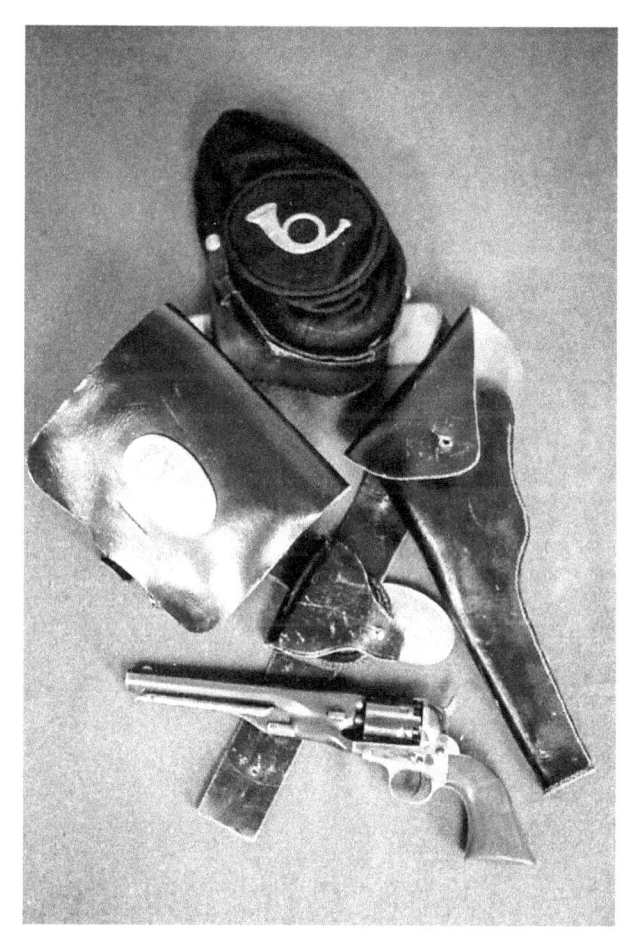

Sources

2nd Tennessee Infantry Regiment (Bates), Google search and Wikipedia
http://freepages.genealogy.rootsweb.ancestry.com/~providence/cw_chap2.htm
http://www.tngenweb.org/civilwar/csainf/bates.html

Confederate Heartland Campaign Map American Civil War June to October 1862
http://americancivilwar.com/statepic/ky/ky009.html
http://americancivilwar.com/campaigns/Confederate_Heartland_Campaign.html

19th Tennessee Infantry Regiment, Google search and Wikipedia
http://en.wikipedia.org/wiki/19th_Tennessee_Infantry
http://www.tngenweb.org/civilwar/csainf/csa19.html
http://dlc.lib.utk.edu/spc/view?docId=tei/0012_003579_000201_0000/0012_003579_000201_0000.xml;brand=default;
http://www.civilwar.org/hallowed-ground-magazine/spring-2010/preserving-kentuckys-battlefields.html

31st Indiana Infantry Regiment, Google search and Wikipedia
http://en.wikipedia.org/wiki/31st_Indiana_Infantry_Regiment
http://www.31stindiana.com/31hist.html
http://ehistory.osu.edu/exhibitions/Regimental/indiana/union/31stIndiana/history

Battle of Richmond, Kentucky, Google search and Wikipedia
http://en.wikipedia.org/wiki/Battle_of_Richmond
http://www.ofsavagefury.com/

Battle of Perryville, Google search and Wikipedia
http://en.wikipedia.org/wiki/Battle_of_Perryville
http://www.civilwar.org/battlefields/perryville.html
http://www.battleofperryville.com/index.html
http://upload.wikimedia.org/wikipedia/commons/9/93/Perryville_1745.png

Cunningham, O. Edward, *Shiloh and the Western Campaign of 1862* (New York, Savas Beatie, 2007).

Confederate Heartland Offensive, Google search and Wikipedia
http://en.wikipedia.org/wiki/Confederate_Heartland_Offensive
http://www.ohiocivilwarcentral.com/entry.php?rec=183
http://www.mycivilwar.com/campaigns/620600.html
http://www.google.com/search?q=Confederate+Heartland+Offensive&ie=utf-8&oe=utf-8&aq=t&rls=org.mozilla:en-US:official&client=firefox-a

Darley, James M., Chief Cartographer, Melville Bell Grosvenor, Editor. "Battlefields of the Civil War with descriptive notes," Atlas Plate 14, April 1961. Compiled and Drawn in the Cartographic Division of The National Geographic Society for The National Geographic Magazine.

Despain, Karen, "Chino Valley woman finds trove of ancestor's letters from Civil War era," The Daily Courier (Prescott Arizona, April 3, 2014).

Johnson, Robert Underwood and Clarence Clough Buel, editors, "Retreat From Gettysburg," Battles and Leaders of the Civil War Volume III (New York, Thomas Yoselooff, 1956).

Nevin, David and Time-Life editors, The Road to Shiloh, Early Battles in the West (Alexandria, Virginia, Time-Life Books, 1983).

Street, James, Jr. and Time-Life editors, The Struggle for Tennessee, Tupelo to Stones River (Alexandria, Virginia, Time-Life Books, 1985).

About the Author,
J. Arthur Moore

J. Arthur Moore is an educator with over 41 years experience in public, private, and independent settings. He is also an amateur photographer and has illustrated his works with his own photographs. In addition to *Blake's Story, Revenge and Forgiveness*, Mr. Moore has written a four-part Civil War historic fiction *Journey into Darkness;* "Heir to Balmawr", a drama for his fifth grade students; a number of short pieces and short stories. His latest release, just prior to *Blake's Story*, is an earlier novel titled *Summer of Two Worlds*, set in Montana Territory in the summer of 1882.

A graduate of Jenkintown High School, just outside of Philadelphia, Pennsylvania, he attended West Chester State College, currently West Chester University. Upon graduation, he joined the Navy and was stationed in Norfolk, Virginia, where he met his wife to be, a widow with four children. Once discharged from the service, he moved to Coatesville,

Pennsylvania, began his teaching career, married and brought his new family to live in a 300-year-old farm house in which the children grew up and married, went their own ways, raised their families to become grandparents themselves.

Retiring after a 42-year career, Mr. Moore has moved to the farming country in Lancaster County, Pennsylvania, where he plans to enjoy the generations of family, time with his model railroad, and time to guide his writings into a new life through publication. It also allows for the opportunity to participate in a local model railroad club as well as time for traveling to Civil War events and presenting at various organizations and events about the boys who were part of that war. He also shares the process of writing and readings from his work, and does book signings at a variety of locations.

Mr. Moore can be reached through the contact page of the website for his books at **www.jarthurmoore.com** with links to its Facebook and Twitter pages; and a boys page focusing on the stories of the boys who served in the Civil War.

More Readers' Comments from Amazon, and an Email

"This book is filled with great characters and a fascinating plot, but the best part is, the story is told from a child's perspective. Luckily, while many of us were children, we were not child soldiers, so it is interesting to see what a child thinks of the war and how a child acts in frightening times like that. Blake's Story really brings you on an exciting journey filled with sadness, happiness, and so much more. It is a great read that I highly recommend to everyone!" **Kojiro Shapier**

"While the Civil War was about one hundred fifty years ago, it's still interesting to learn about. I have read many books on the subject, non-fiction, fiction, and this may be the most unique. Many of the soldiers in the Civil War were just boys and this story takes you on one boys journey through the biggest bloodbath in American History. It's a great book and a must read!" **Andrew James**

"I hope my children never have to experience active war time while they are young, like the narrator of Blake's Story. The Civil War was a definite time of unrest for our nation, and this book gives us a first-hand account of what it was like to be a child soldier during the bloodiest battle our soil has seen in recent times. Great characters and empathetic situations bring up a host of emotions in the reader, which is what any good book should do. Excellent read for everyone." **N.A.**

"War is heartbreaking for people of any age, but it's especially tough on children. During the Civil War, many children were called upon to fight for their country and it left an indelible impression on everyone involved. Blake's Story is a tale unique to the times, but speaks of truths we all still struggle with in the themes everyone can understand - love, revenge, forgiveness and heartache. The book is well-written and gripping, throwing you through a portal in time straight to the battlefield. A devouring read, and highly recommended." **Mary**

"Innocence and Empathy. Love and Sacrifice. The gripping plot of this book has been so designed that it takes anyone reading it on a whirlwind ride into the details of the above mentioned human emotions. The life of a boy soldier, horrible. J. Arthur Moore successfully details out a child's perception of war and the way he reacts to the horrific bloodbaths in his own innocent immature ways. The age of playing with wooden toy guns suddenly becomes a pathetic attempt for survival.. I highly recommend this book if you want something to read and feel good about. Something that will connect to your emotions and something that will tell you to hate war." **Simantini Mohanty**

Dear Mr. Moore,

    I found your book very interesting and educational. I have learned a lot about the Civil War through your books. I find them much more exciting than a dry history textbook. It was inspiring to see how Blake was bitter toward the enemy for killing his father, but in the end he actually met the man who killed his father and forgave him. It is a story of bitterness and anger, which turns into forgiveness and friendship. **Isaac Sassa, age 14**